Rose's eyes were closing now. In another few seconds she would be asleep. Maybe she should relieve Yannis of the burden on his shoulder. But something told her he was quite comfortable with the arrangement, and she didn't want to speak until Rose was asleep.

They sat together in a companionable silence that was broken only by the sound of the sea close beside them below the rocky promontory. Cathy moved her gaze to her daughter, who was now peacefully sleeping with her small head cradled against Yannis's shoulder.

Yannis saw Cathy looking anxiously at her daughter. Gently he eased the child down to a more comfortable position, cradled in the crook of his left arm. He smiled across the table, wondering why he felt so comfortable here with this mother and baby.

This was what life would have been like if… If only he… No! He mustn't torment himself by going down that road again. Just enjoy this simple, pleasurable feeling that was stealing over him—if he would let it.

He forced himself to relax again. 'Rose is sound asleep now, Cathy, so don't worry about her.'

She stopped herself just in time, avoiding the question she'd wanted to ask. Looking across at Yannis now, with her daughter cradled in the crook of his arm, she thought he looked like the perfect father.

Margaret Barker has enjoyed a variety of interesting careers. A State Registered Nurse and qualified teacher, she holds a degree in French and Linguistics, and is a Licentiate of the Royal Academy of Music. As a full-time writer, Margaret says, 'Writing is my most interesting career, because it fits perfectly into family life. Sadly, my husband died of cancer in 2006, but I still live in our idyllic sixteenth-century house near the East Anglian coast. Our grown-up children have flown the nest, but they often fly back again, bringing their own young families with them for wonderful weekend and holiday reunions.'

Recent titles by the same author:

GREEK DOCTOR CLAIMS HIS BRIDE
THE FATHERHOOD MIRACLE

A FATHER
FOR BABY ROSE

BY
MARGARET BARKER

First published in Great Britain 2010
Large Print edition 2011
Harlequin Mills & Boon Limited,
Eton House, 18-24 Paradise Road,
Richmond, Surrey TW9 1SR

© Margaret Barker 2010

ISBN: 978 0 263 21713 1

Harlequin Mills & Boon policy is to use papers that are natural, renewable and recyclable products and made from wood grown in sustainable forests. The logging and manufacturing process conform to the legal environmental regulations of the country of origin.

Printed and bound in Great Britain
by CPI Antony Rowe, Chippenham, Wiltshire

A FATHER
FOR BABY ROSE

CHAPTER ONE

CATHY pushed the buggy past the vibrant tavernas edging the harbour, which hummed and buzzed with early evening revellers. Little Rose, squashed against her pillows in the buggy, was leaning forward now so she could point out something of interest that she wanted Mummy to see.

Cathy put her foot on the brake and went round to the front of the buggy, smiling down at her daughter.

"What is it, darling?"

Ah, yes, now she saw it. Rose loved cats. The black and white cat was now mingling with a group of people strolling along the harbour. The nearest woman to Rose's buggy bent down to look at the small girl.

"*Kali spera*," she said to Cathy as she smiled down at her daughter. "*Posseleni*?"

Rose chuckled but didn't reply to the woman who was asking her name.

"My daughter is only ten months old," Cathy explained in Greek. "She's called Rose."

"Horaya!"

As the woman hurried away to catch up with her friends Cathy repeated the compliment under her breath. *"Horaya!"* She didn't know whether the woman considered the name or her daughter to be beautiful but whatever it was she was right on both counts.

She paused to look up at the beautiful evening sky, not a sign of a cloud, the golden shades of the advancing twilight mingling with the seemingly endless blue that merged with the lighter colour of the sea. What a difference eighteen months had made! The last time she'd been here on the island she hadn't even known that she was actually going to be a mother. And then when she'd found out!

She drew in her breath as she remembered the shock, horror, her awful, mixed, muddled emotional reactions. How could she have had such dreadful ideas? She swallowed hard. How different her life would be now without Rose, the centre of her universe. There would be no meaning to it at all, apart from her medical career. But even that paled into insignificance now that she was a mother.

Eighteen months ago she'd come out to Ceres to attend her cousin Tanya's wedding, so happy to get away for a while, still licking her wounds and feeling the awful despair of another failed relationship. When Tanya had suggested she apply for the temporary appointment of doctor that would be available when she and her husband Manolis went on honeymoon, she'd jumped at the chance.

But two weeks later, back at home in Leeds, discovering she was pregnant had changed everything. She still had to suffer the awful pangs of despair at the fact that Dave had gone back to a wife she hadn't known existed. Coupled with the morning sickness that had set in with a vengeance, she'd withdrawn her application for the temporary post at Ceres hospital.

When Rose had been a few months old Tanya had phoned to say she and Manolis were taking a six-month sabbatical from Ceres hospital to work in Australia and there would be a vacant post for her if she wanted to apply. She'd got a second chance! Tanya had asked if she would like to stay in their house and she'd even arranged child care for Rose. She could make a fresh start at last and concentrate on her number one priority, Rose.

Looking down at her beautiful daughter, she could feel her heart lifting at the thought that they were going to be fine out here. Life was beginning to take shape again.

Involuntarily, she increased her stride, now desperate to get away from the evening crowds by the harbour, yearning for the peace and calm of the next bay where all would be quiet and she could sit down at a table outside the final taverna, which she remembered from the times her mother had taken her there as a child was always quiet.

She needed to watch the sun setting whilst chatting to Rose in Greek or English as her own mother had done with her. It didn't matter which. Rose was learning both languages as she had when her mother had brought her here every holiday to "pick up Greek" from her cousins and the children she played with.

Later, while at medical school, she'd taken Greek lessons with a private tutor who'd helped her sort out the grammar and linguistic rules. He had also been a retired Greek doctor, which had been a help when she'd made sure she was conversant with Greek medical terminology. She'd always hoped she might have a chance to use it. Never had she thought things would turn out as they had!

The buggy was rattling alarmingly now and not just the gentle groaning of an ancient model that should have been scrapped long ago. She tried to ignore it as she pushed hard against the rough cobblestones. Seconds later it ground to a jolting halt. What now?

She hadn't wanted to borrow it from Grandma Anna's vast array of baby equipment because it had obviously seen years of service. But Anna had been very persuasive, telling her that it would be difficult to get a taxi down from Chorio, the upper town, to Yialos, the area around the harbour. The hourly bus would be overcrowded and with standing room only. Much better to push Rose in the buggy down the *Kali Strata*.

Cathy knelt down to take a look at the loose wheel that was now firmly stuck in a deep crevice in the cobblestones. Rose leaned over the side and stroked Cathy's long blond hair as she struggled to extricate the wheel, gurgling all the while, obviously desperate to communicate her own thoughts on the situation!

"Can I help you?"

The deep masculine voice startled her. She adjusted her sunglasses as she squinted up at the tall figure outlined in the dying rays of the low-lying sun.

"Oh, it's you! For a moment I hadn't recognised you in…in your er…casual gear, Dr Karavolis."

"Please call me Yannis."

That wasn't what he'd said that afteroon when she'd disturbed him whilst he'd been operating in Theatre! His eyes above the mask had carried a definite expression of irritation as she'd pushed open the swing door, taken a peek and then hurried away.

Holding onto the buggy handle, she stood up so as not to feel inferior to Dr Karavolis for the second time in one day. Tanya had told her when she'd been contemplating coming out to work at the Ceres hospital that she might find Yannis Karavolis difficult to understand on a personal level. She'd explained that his wife had died in a tragic accident over three years ago and he didn't seem to have yet recovered. He was an excellent doctor, apparently, but made no effort to socialise.

"Let me take a look at that wheel."

He bent down just as she was standing up and

she felt his arm accidentally brush the side of her breast as she attempted to rise from her crouching position as elegantly as possible. For a second it startled her, the feel of a man's arm against her body. The hint of masculine scent as he crouched down. She had thought she was now totally immune to instant attraction. But she couldn't ignore the heightening of her senses, the excitement of being in close contact with a man, the probably imagined increase in her pulse rate.

Heavens above! She would have to get out more so that she could apply her new rules to every encounter with the opposite sex. She'd had her fingers burned so many times before that she wasn't going to ever—repeat, ever—take another chance with a man. However handsome—and Dr Karavolis was decidedly handsome from where she was now standing. If she wasn't now so world weary and experienced she might have considered a little dalliance with this man who'd literally just dropped by so suddenly.

Rose was now giggling, having stuck out a chubby, dimpled hand to grasp a clump of the helpful doctor's thick black hair.

Cathy, glanced anxiously down at the crouching Yannis. Their eyes met. For a moment she felt a definite flutter of excitement. Yes, that's what it was. Just a simple flutter but enough to make her think that this man must have been quite something in his younger days; before tragedy had turned him into a working zombie.

It was a good thing that she'd given up on the difficult male species or she might at that fleeting moment have found herself advancing her embryonic ideas into something exciting.

His eyes were dark brown, sultry, vulnerable. She'd had time to notice that before he bent down once more to his task.

"Gently, Rose," Cathy said in Greek. "You must be careful not to hurt Dr Karavolis"

Rose giggled on, completely ignoring her mother's instructions.

"You're teaching your daughter Greek? That's good."

"Oh, she'll pick it up like I had to when I came out here for holidays and my cousin Tanya and all the other children used to make fun of me. I soon learned out of self-preservation, I can tell you."

Yannis gave one more tug at the wheel and removed it from the deeply sunken crevice between the cobblestones.

"Here's the wheel, but unfortunately it's come unstuck from the buggy," he said, gravely. He pulled himself to his full height, holding the wheel in one hand and making sure the buggy remained upright with the other.

Cathy looked up at him. "Well, er…thank you, anyway. I suppose…"

"Look, I was just going to have a drink and watch the sunset so…"

"Great minds think alike. I mean, we were just…"

"Please, why don't you join me?"

He couldn't imagine why he'd just said that! Company was the last thing he needed after his long, tiring day at the hospital. Especially another doctor…and a child…

"Both of us?"

He took a deep breath. "Well, we can hardly ask Rose to sit it out in her broken pushchair."

He was already unbuckling the seat belt and lifting the delighted baby up into his arms. Something about the way he held her daughter told Cathy he adored babies, children in general.

She wondered, fleetingly, if he had children being looked after by a doting grandmother back in Athens, which Tanya had told her had been where he'd been working before he'd come here. Better not ask. She didn't want to upset the fragile ambience that was building up between them.

Carefully holding Rose, whose fingers, had now transferred from his hair to his ears, he pushed the wrecked pushchair to the side of the path and led the way to the taverna that occupied the rocky peninsula at the beginning of this quiet bay.

The owner came out to the table Yannis had selected, beaming all over his face. He was carrying two glasses half-full of colourless liquid.

"I saw you struggling with that buggy," he said in Greek. "You need a drink, *ghiatro.*"

So, the owner knew Yannis was a doctor. Probably this was Yannis's hideaway when he was off duty, searching for solitude.

"Efharisto, Michaeli." Yannis proceeded to introduce Cathy as Dr Catherine Meredith.

So Yannis had found the time between operations to check that she'd signed in with the admin department today. Otherwise she doubted whether her arrival on the island had registered with him. Certainly, no one had been expecting her to turn up unannounced today. The staff in the small admin department had told her she was expected to start work tomorrow but she could have a look around if she wanted to. That had been when she'd made her solitary tour of the hospital and barged into Theatre.

She picked up her glass. Realising the clear liquid was ouzo, Cathy decided to ask Michaelis for some water to dilute it. *"Nero, parakalor."*

"You're sure you're happy with ouzo?" Yannis asked as Michaelis disappeared inside the taverna to get the water.

She smiled. "When in Rome…or rather on Ceres…it's best to go with the flow. I prefer wine but I don't want to hurt Michaelis's feelings. He obviously knows you very well."

"Oh, yes, we go back a long way. I've got a house further along this bay, on the shoreline near Nimborio. This is my bolt hole at the end of the day."

"I thought it might be."

Michaelis brought a bottle of water. Yannis, expertly holding the tired child against his shoulder, leaned across and topped up Cathy's glass.

"Thank you."

He raised his glass towards her. *"Yamas!"*

"Yamas!"

Rose's eyes were closing now. In another few

seconds she would be asleep. Maybe she should relieve him of the burden on his shoulder. But something told her he was quite comfortable with the arrangement and she didn't want to speak until Rose was asleep.

They sat together in companionable silence that was broken only by the sound of the sea close beside them below the rocky promontory. Cathy found her eyes, protected by her sunglasses, drawn towards the sun that was slipping slowly behind the mountain, casting a shadow over their table. She moved her gaze to her daughter, who was now peacefully sleeping with her small head cradled against Yannis's shoulder.

Yannis saw Cathy looking anxiously at her daughter. Gently he eased the child down to a more comfortable position, cradled in the crook of his left arm. He smiled across the table, wondering why he felt so comfortable here with this mother and baby. It was a whole new experience and not something he'd expected to enjoy like this. He could feel it soothing his jangled nerves.

This was what life would have been like if... if only he... No! He mustn't torment himself by going down that road again. Just enjoy this simple, pleasurable feeling that was stealing over him—if he would let it.

He forced himself to relax again. "Rose is sound asleep now, Cathy, so don't worry about her. Would you prefer a glass of wine?"

"Well, only if…"

He tipped his ouzo glass and finished the fiery liquid in one swift gulp. "So would I."

Usually he sat, watching the sunset, sipping his ouzo slowly before ordering supper and a glass of wine, always reminding himself that he needed a clear head for his work the following morning. He'd no idea where this reckless feeling had come from but he was suddenly feeling in party mood. It had been a long time since he'd felt like this.

Michaelis, who was obviously watching from his seat just inside the door, came hurrying across and after a discussion about whether the wine was to be red or white he disappeared again, bringing out a tray with a selection of mezes and a bottle of white wine.

"We Greeks usually like to eat something if we're drinking wine," Yannis explained, pointing out the different small dishes of taramasalata, squid, calamari and olives. "But, then, you've obviously spent a lot of time in the Greek community so I don't need to tell you all this. I vaguely remember meeting you at Tanya and Manolis's wedding. So you're Tanya's cousin?"

"Yes, our mothers were sisters. My mother was keen to bring me over to Ceres after her sister married Dr Sotiris and came to live out here. Every holiday she would bring me here so that I could learn the language and absorb the Greek culture. I'd always hoped that one day I would have the opportunity to come and work out here."

Yannis leaned across the table and poured more wine into Cathy's glass. She'd hardly touched the ouzo but seemed to be enjoying the wine.

"I didn't know you were planning to start a family when I last saw you."

Cathy raised an eyebrow. "Neither did I! I'd just ended a relationship and didn't know I was pregnant. Tanya had just suggested I apply for the temporary four-week post they needed to fill at the hospital while she and Manolis were away on honeymoon. I'd decided I'd go for it, but when I found I was pregnant I withdrew my application.

"Difficult, I imagine. I'm sorry the relationship ended."

"I'm not! It was far too complicated. But I can't imagine life without my wonderful daughter. She's the most special thing that's ever happened to me. Did you…?"

She stopped herself just in time to avoid the question she'd wanted to ask. Looking across at Yannis now, with her daughter cradled in the crook of his arm, he looked like the perfect father.

He filled the awkward silence that ensued. "You were going to ask if my wife and I had children, weren't you?"

She cringed inwardly. "Well…"

"The answer is no. It…it wasn't to be."

He'd managed to refer to that most poignant period of his life without faltering and that was a step in the right direction. He hadn't told the whole truth but that would be a step too far. He couldn't bring himself to even think about it.

Taking a sip of his wine, he tried to blot out everything that had happened on that fateful day when his life had changed for ever. He put the glass down on the table. Looking across at the sympathetic expression on Cathy's face, he suddenly found his tongue loosening as if he was in an involuntary state of relaxation.

"My wife was killed in a car crash." He didn't need to say anything more but the guilt that always rose up inside him when he thought about the circumstances surrounding her death—which was often—was nagging him to confess more to this obviously sympathetic colleague.

"I often wonder…" He paused. He didn't need to go on. He didn't need to torment himself further. "I often wonder if I could have prevented it."

There, he'd said it out loud; revealed the horrible nightmare that returned over and over again when he reviewed what had happened.

The child stirred against him. In some ways he found the small body tucked against the crook of his arm very comforting. His thoughts returned to the present situation. He waited for the agony of his confession to make him feel awful but he felt strangely comforted to have shared this with Cathy—and the sleeping baby, although, thank goodness, the little mite couldn't hear him.

Cathy was simply looking across the table with a bewildered expression on her lovely face as she stretched out her hand towards him. With his free hand he took hold of Cathy's and felt a sympathetic, most welcome squeeze of her fingers.

Something like an electric shock—a pleasant one—travelled up his arm.

For a few seconds they remained like that, simply looking at each other. She thought she could discern the tears that threatened behind his eyes but doubted that he'd ever allowed them to fall since whatever dreadful tragedy had taken place. She could tell this man was made of stern stuff. Strong backbone, wouldn't give in to self-pity but also found it hard to communicate the grief that was holding him back from getting on with a normal life.

Yannis took his hand away and leaned back in his chair, taking care not to disturb Rose. "I'm sorry to talk about the car crash like this. I've never discussed it with anybody before. I can't think why…"

"Maybe you should."

"Should what?" He looked alarmed.

"Discuss it with somebody. Me, for a start. It always helps if you talk a problem over with somebody."

He was silent as he thought of all the aspects of the tragedy surrounding Maroula's death. No, he couldn't discuss it openly with this woman he hardly knew. He shouldn't even have got so close to her that he felt he could trust her with his feelings. He couldn't think what had come over him. In a way it was a betrayal of trust to Maroula's memory. What had happened was part of his life with his wife and no one else. And yet...

"You don't have to discuss it with me," Cathy said. "It's entirely up to you. I would, however, be the soul of discretion so if you ever think it would help you to..."

"Thanks, I'll remember that."

His tone was firm, final, signifying they should move on. He was already regretting the fact that he'd allowed himself to talk about his beloved Maroula with someone he hardly knew. Discussing his feelings of guilt—something he'd never spoken about out loud before—wasn't going to bring her back.

Anyway, he was settled in his bachelor ways now. The future was mapped out and he didn't want to become close enough to any other person to allow them to break through the emotional barrier he'd erected around himself. He needed to retreat behind his safe barrier again. Back to Maroula. He was being unfaithful to her memory, something he'd vowed would never happen.

Little Rose wriggled in Yannis's arms, rubbing

her chubby fists against her eyes before she opened them and stared up at him. A big smile spread across her face.

Cathy stood up and moved round the table, holding out her arms towards her daughter.

Rose lifted her arms towards Cathy.

Yannis couldn't help smiling as he handed over the little girl. "There you go, Rose. What a good little girl you've been."

Michaelis came out of the taverna to see if he could get something for the baby.

"I've got some fruit juice in her baby cup," Cathy said, sitting down once more on her seat, baby on one arm as she searched through her shoulder-bag. "Here it is."

Rose was already halfway across the table, reaching for a piece of calamari and dunking it into the taramasalata.

"Bravo!" Yannis said. "Rose is hungry."

"She loves calamari, as you can see." Cathy wiped a paper napkin round her daughter's face to remove some of the taramasalata. Rose pushed her mother's hand away as she savoured the delicious taste in her mouth.

"I've prepared some lamb souvlaki on the barbecue," Michaelis said, looking enquiringly from Yannis to Cathy. "Shall I bring them now?"

The lamb kebabs were delicious. Rose sucked on a tiny piece of tender meat then gummed it for a little while before depositing it on Cathy's plate.

"She likes to try everything."

Yannis smiled. "That's good. By the time you've been here—remind me, how long is it you're working at the hospital?"

"Six months. Tanya and Manolis have been offered a six-month sabbatical, if you remember."

"Yes, yes. I remember signing your contract now. You were interviewed in London, I remember. Manolis has put me in charge of the day-to-day running of the medical and surgical side of the hospital while he's away but I leave the paperwork to our efficient administration team. I knew you were coming in to work tomorrow but when you arrived briefly in Theatre this morning I couldn't think who you were. Sorry if I was less than welcoming. I was in the middle of a difficult operation and—'

"Oh, please. I hadn't realised that the theatre was in use. My fault."

"I'll take time to show you around tomorrow."

"Thank you."

Rose was now crushing a potato chip against her mouth before opening it and demolishing it with her four tiny white teeth. She wiped her hands over her blond curly hair and grinned happily.

"I think it's time for me to take Rose home," Cathy said, reaching for another paper napkin. "I've got the numbers of the taxi drivers in my mobile so I'll see who's free to come and get us."

The brief twilight had faded already, she noticed as she punched in the first number on her list. That number was engaged. She tried the next on the list and was lucky this time.

"Theo will be with us in ten minutes," she said as she closed her mobile.

"Good. I'm glad you're not going to attempt to walk back. I'll take your buggy home with me and ask Petros, the man who helps me in the garden, to see if he can mend it. He can mend most things."

Except broken hearts, Cathy thought as she smiled her thanks. It was so obvious to her that Yannis's heart would need a lot of tender loving care from a good woman. She certainly wasn't the person to do it because she needed to keep her own life on track. Whoever took on the mending of Yannis's heart would have a difficult job breaking down the barriers he'd built around himself.

She reminded herself firmly that whatever it was that that Yannis needed, she shouldn't feel obliged to try and provide it. After all, she was always the one left wanting when she was barrelled into trying to smooth things along for people. Besides which, she wasn't here to get too involved with another man, let alone a colleague she was going to have to work intimately with for the next six months.

Out loud she told Yannis that she didn't think Grandma Anna would need the pushchair for a while.

"Rose is her youngest baby at the moment. Tanya told me she was getting withdrawal symptoms now that they were taking baby Jack over to Australia. Anna told me today she's lost count of how many babies she's cared for over the years."

"She's an amazing woman. But you must still find it hard, being a single parent and working full time as a doctor."

"I'm very lucky. In England, my mother takes care of Rose when I'm working and here I've got

Anna. I wanted to spend a short time away from Rose today to see how she would get on with Anna. She absolutely adores her already so I won't have to worry about her when I'm working."

"So why did you want to bring Rose out with you this evening?"

"I wanted to spend some quality time with her. Every mother's guilt trip, I suppose. Working away from home and leaving her baby in the care of someone else."

Yannis swallowed hard. "Guilt is a terrible affliction. We all suffer from it at times."

She saw the worried look on his handsome face and wished she could conjure up that wonderful smile he'd had just a short time ago. She'd noticed the flash of his strong white teeth, the curve of his full, sensuous lips, the vulnerable expression in his dark, brooding, brown eyes.

She gave herself another mental talking-to. She wasn't in the dating market any more. Neither, it seemed, was Yannis—wise man! Never again! Not after the disastrous relationships she'd suffered over the years. Life was going to be very good if she avoided meaningful relationships.

"I think this is your taxi coming along the coast road."

She gathered Rose up into her arms. *"Kali nichta, Yannis,"*

"Kali nichta, Cathy. I…" He hesitated. "I look forward to seeing you again tomorrow."

CHAPTER TWO

CATHY waited until she could hear Rose breathing that easy, steady rhythmic way that usually indicated her daughter was well and truly out for the count—for a few hours anyway. Barefoot, she walked backwards so she could keep an eye on her daughter, just in case she'd misjudged the situation.

She propped open the door then looked back to make sure she'd put the teddy-bear books that Rose loved so much at the end of her cot, where she would see them if she woke up early. With any luck, as had happened a few times recently back home in England, she just might become entranced by one of the pictures and give her sleeping mother a few more minutes of blissful oblivion.

Was she being over-cautious, over-anxious, over the top in her solitary state as a single parent? If she had a husband or lover waiting in bed for her now, would she be taking so much time? That would depend on the man in question. Sitting down at her dressing table, she confronted the image of an exhausted, sleep-deprived thirty-one-year-old mum with developing crow's feet at the corners of her tired blue eyes.

What an evening! she told herself as she wiped off the bronzer that she'd applied earlier in the evening so as not to frighten the tourists with her unseasonal pallor. It may only be April but out here on Ceres the season was already in full swing following the Easter festivities, and there were lots of healthy-looking people tramping over the hills and lying on the beaches.

She'd never imagined that she would end the day in the company of Yannis Karavolis who, although technically in charge of the hospital, hadn't seemed to know who she was when she'd arrived. She'd obviously been infinitely forgettable when she'd met him eighteen months ago at Tanya's wedding, whereas he… She felt embarrassed now that she'd been attracted to him as soon as she'd seen him skulking—perhaps that wasn't the word, more kind of hiding—in the kitchen so he wouldn't have to mingle with the revellers.

She'd split up with Dave two weeks before, and

had already been licking her wounds and vowing never to get interested in a man again. But there had been something appealing about Yannis tonight. His total vulnerability. His obvious unshakeable devotion to his deceased wife. Tanya had just told her about his wife's tragic death, she remembered.

She realised now that if she were to fancy him—which she didn't…well, no, she mustn't! But if she were to even think of him as sexy, which he was, handsome, interesting to be with, yes, but only when he wasn't thinking about his wife.

Now, that would be the obstacle. Yannis's total obsession with the unattainable. His wife was dead, but yet, in his mind, she obviously lived on, set on a pedestal where nothing and nobody could ever replace her. So in a way, if anybody did try to take her down from the pedestal, somebody—not herself, oh, no! But just supposing she were to allow her feelings of attraction towards Yannis to develop into…

But she wasn't going to! However, if she hadn't decided never to have a meaningful relationship or even a fling with another man she just might, having imagined herself to be attracted to Yannis, forget her single-woman plan and have another go at romance.

She picked up the hairbrush and brushed her hair vigorously. It would be a stupid thing to do but she was renowned for making stupid decisions—or rather non-decisions, drifting into disastrous situations that started out as fun and ended in tears.

And this hypothetical idea that she'd just dreamed up would most certainly end in tears! The goddess-like wife would always be there with them. And Cathy had played second fiddle long enough. Dave had told her he was separated from his wife and waiting for the divorce to come through. And idiot that she was, she'd believed him. The long business trips abroad he'd had to make away from her! She hadn't questioned them because she had been in love and, therefore, that meant she trusted him implicitly.

What an idiot she could be! For a whole year she'd believed everything he'd told her. She'd been taken in by every single lie he'd told her.

It was the truth she couldn't believe!

That awful Saturday morning when he'd turned up and announced his divorce wasn't going through as planned. Well...sheepish expression on his face…to be honest, they hadn't got around to planning it. Actually, he was still theoretically living at home. He and his wife had decided they were going to make a go of it. Purely for the sake of the kids, you know. His wife didn't know about Cathy so he'd be truly grateful if she would keep it that way.

Mind you, if it were up to him…blah, blah, blah… She'd stopped listening to him by this time as she remembered the lonely Christmas she'd spent because he'd told her he had to go and stay with his sick mother. The numerous weekends when he'd had to fly away on business.

She put down the hairbrush and stared into the mirror again, this time seeing the face of a very gullible woman who never learned by her mistakes. But at least this time she'd learned. It would be the same kind of scenario if she chose to have any kind of dalliance with Yannis Karavolis. She would play second fiddle again to the perfect wife who could do no wrong. Yannis's wife may not be with them in the flesh but she would certainly be with them in spirit.

She forced herself to grin at the picture of desolation she posed in the mirror. "Don't take yourself so seriously," she told herself. "It's not as if you're remotely attracted to the man so the situation isn't going to arise."

And with that she crawled between the cool sheets and tried to fall asleep. The fact that she tossed and turned for half the night was put down to the fact that she was suffering from jet-lag. Towards dawn she decided to get up and finish unpacking and sorting out her bedroom. At the first squeak from Rose she was in there, smiling welcomingly at her daughter, reaching out her arms for a cuddle.

In his bedroom overlooking the wide inlet of moonlit sea in Nimborio bay, Yannis was also finding it hard to sleep. He hadn't expected to enjoy the evening when he'd invited Cathy and her little daughter Rose to join him for a drink. He'd certainly never envisaged they would all have supper together. And now it was time to admit to himself that he hadn't felt so alive since before Maroula had died.

He flung the sheet away from him. It was too hot to be covered tonight. He ran a hand down the side of his naked body as he experienced a feeling of strength flowing through him. It was a good feeling, but the feeling was also tinged with confusion. Was it guilt, this awful feeling now that he shouldn't be able to enjoy life without Maroula? He supposed it was. He didn't really think he deserved to enjoy himself like that in the company of an unattached young woman.

It wasn't as if he'd flirted with her, because he hadn't. But she might have misinterpreted his friendliness as an ulterior motive, mightn't she? She might have thought he fancied her in a sexual way. Well, actually, if he was truly honest with himself, he did! And that was something he couldn't hide from himself.

That was another thing he'd discovered tonight. Looking across at Cathy, who was undoubtedly very attractive, he'd felt himself almost if not actually, physically moved. And that hadn't happened since Maroula had died. He'd made sure that if he was in the company of an attractive woman he held a tight rein on his sexual emotions.

He'd lived like a monk for over three years. But tonight he'd felt himself drawn towards Cathy in a way that he couldn't dismiss. Was it because he sensed that she was also trying to survive, that she was vulnerable like he was? He was attracted by her beauty, her warmth, her forthrightness and the fact that because she was a stranger she had the distance needed to be able to ask direct questions.

Whatever it was, he hadn't been able to stop himself from allowing these long-lost feelings deep down inside him to come back.

But should he let them? Hadn't he vowed that Maroula was his lifelong soul-mate? She was no longer here but he was. And what about all the promises he'd made after she'd died? He was going to make it up to her. She'd been cut off unnecessarily in her prime and he'd pledged to spend the rest of his life devoted to her memory.

He found himself beginning to get drowsy at long last. His last thoughts as he drifted off were about how he would love to have Cathy beside him here in his bed. Because his wicked physical longings were becoming unbearable. He doubted he would be able to resist the temptation of her wonderful seductive body. The trouble was that if he gave in he would never be able to forgive himself.

Cathy hurried down the *Kali Strata,* aware that she wouldn't be able to reach the hospital in time. Having hardly slept all night, she'd spent too much time giving Rose breakfast, washing and dressing her, playing with her and finally taking her to Anna's house.

Breathlessly she hurried into the hospital. A flash of recognition registered on the reception-ist's face as she leaned forward.

"Dr Karavolis would like to see you in his office, Dr Meredith."

Cathy smiled. At least she was expected today. "Thank you. Which way...?"

The receptionist pointed. "Straight along the corridor. It's the last door you come to."

As she hurried down the long corridor, Cathy wondered if Yannis had chosen to be right at the end so that he would have a quiet bolt hole when he needed it.

"Come in!"

She pushed open the door. Yannis was seated at a large, imposing desk, staring at a computer screen. He stood up and came round the desk, taking one of the two armchairs and indicating she should sit in the other.

She sat down, wondering why she was feeling so awkward now. Was it that she'd fantasised about him so much in the night and now, seeing this tired-looking man with the serious face, she was realising that she'd misjudged the situation completely? They'd simply had a drink together and eaten some food because they'd been hungry. End of story, thank goodness!

"Did you get home all right last night?" he asked gravely.

"Yes, the taxi took me to the end of the street. How about you?"

"I live very near Michaelis's taverna. A short walk. I asked Petros, my gardener, to collect your buggy this morning and see if he could mend it."

Silence, the ticking of a clock in the background, the hum of the computer. Cathy cleared her throat. "Where would you like me to start work today?"

He picked up a file from his desk. "I've mapped out your duties, which will vary from day to day. All the information you should need is in here. Today we have an open clinic in Outpatients. I've alerted the midwife who's working in the obstetrics section that you'll be joining her shortly. She'll be delighted to see you. Women doctors are always popular with our obstetric patients and at the moment one of our ladies is on maternity leave. Don't worry, we've got plenty of medical staff at the moment so there's plenty of back-up.

It's later in the tourist season that we begin to find ourselves short-staffed. April is a good month to start—apart from Easter."

"What went wrong at Easter?"

For a moment she saw him relax his tight facial muscles and a hint of a smile appeared on his decidedly sexy lips. She felt a pang of interest once more. Something she shouldn't be feeling as she listened to Dr Karavolis explaining the workings of the hospital.

"What didn't go wrong?" He stretched out his long legs in front of him as he visibly relaxed.

She couldn't help noticing the expensive cut of his lightweight suit. The silk-lined jacket was hung over the back of his desk chair and the trousers he was wearing were just tight enough to make him look sexy even though the suit was of a formal design.

She waited for him to elaborate. "Easter celebrations on Ceres last more than a week. Fireworks are set off at every opportunity, and as you know they can cause havoc. Our casualty department was dealing with injuries on a round-the-clock basis."

He stood up, possibly to signify that it was time

to start work. She clutched her file as she moved towards the door.

"I'll come along to see you during the course of the morning," he said as he reached ahead of her to open the door.

She smiled up at him as he held the door open. "Thank you…er…Thank you."

Her hesitation was because she'd no idea what she should call him when they were on duty so she moved swiftly away, back towards Reception.

She could feel a quickening of her pulse rate. Was he going to have this effect on her when they were actually working together? If so, she'd have to get a grip on her emotions.

Yannis remained with the door open, watching Cathy walking away. He'd managed to maintain a professional attitude, which he intended to maintain while on duty. But he had no idea how he was going to handle off-duty situations. He could, of course, make sure that he didn't meet up with her again in an off-duty situation. But having experienced the warmth of an evening spent with Cathy and Rose, he didn't think that was an option. He would just have to be careful when he was with them and not allow the situation to get out of hand.

He closed the door and returned to his computer, staring at the list of surgical operations he had to schedule. It was a long time since he'd felt emotionally confused like this and it was playing havoc with his concentration.

Yannis's decision to be careful came almost at the same time as Cathy got a similar idea firmly fixed in her mind. She was now following the sign above the corridor directing her to Outpatients. Having found the obstetrics section, she was immediately introduced to the midwife in charge.

Sister Maria welcomed her warmly as she went into the treatment room and explained the case history of the patient she was looking after. Cathy smiled down at the patient as she listened.

"Ariadne is a model patient," Maria said in Greek.

The patient smiled. "Only if you say so, Sister."

Cathy looked down at Ariadne. "I hope you don't mind me coming in halfway through the examination. I'm Cathy Meredith, very new here, but I spent a lot of time in Obstetrics when I was working in an English hospital."

"Your Greek is very good, Doctor."

"I've spent a lot of time over here and I have Greek cousins who made fun of me so much when I was a child that I had no option but to pick up as much Greek as I could."

Maria and Ariadne laughed and there was a good, friendly feel between all of them. Cathy always liked to break the ice when she was working. Tense patients were more difficult to take care of.

A young nurse came hurrying into the room, requesting the immediate attention of Sister Maria in the next cubicle. Maria excused herself.

"These are Ariadne's notes, Cathy, and she understands everything that's going on. She used to be a nurse before she started her family."

"Would you like to tell me about your family, Ariadne?" Cathy asked, glancing briefly at the notes.

"These twins will be numbers four and five in the family," Ariadne said, unable to hide the pride she was feeling as she patted her sizeable bump. "We intended to have four children but we were both delighted when I found out we were expecting twins. The more the merrier, my husband says. He wheeled me into hospital and then he went to do some shopping for me. He'll be back soon. I'm not allowed to drive any more and I have to use a wheelchair outside home."

Cathy glanced briefly at the case notes again. "Ariadne, tell me about the day you discovered you had symphysis pubis. It says in the notes that it was a sudden realisation. What actually happened?"

"I'd had a busy day, got the children to bed, cooked supper and then sat at the table with my husband, who'd just got back from a business meeting. He told me to sit still and let him wait on me during the meal. I suppose I was probably sitting for about half an hour. Then, as I stood up and tried to take a step I felt my pelvic bones split open. It was excrutiating. Thank goodness, Demetrius was with me! He got me straight into hospital and they gave me strong painkillers."

"It's a condition that's not uncommon in women carrying more than one baby, Ariadne," Cathy said in a sympathetic tone. "Especially among those who've had a number of births in a short period of time like you have with your first three children. So, I see you were referred to our orthopaedic specialist, who made the diagnosis."

"It was such a relief to find out what was happening. I felt as if somebody had put a sword inside me. I will recover, won't I, Cathy?"

"Yes, you will. Your ligaments, which stretch

naturally during pregnancy and childbirth, have become too loose to hold the pelvis together. But you were given steroid injections, which tighten everything up, weren't you? And I expect you were told to rest."

"I didn't move! I don't go out any more except for my hospital appointment once a week. My mother lives nearby and my husband tries to work from home as much as possible."

"Well, you seem to be doing all the right things. I see your twins are due in July."

"It can't come quick enough for any of us! I've been told I'll be delivered by Caesarean section."

"Yes. A natural birth would put too much strain on the pelvis. But the policy here at Ceres hospital is for operations of this nature to be transferred to the larger hospital on Rhodes. Minor operations are scheduled in for our hospital but most major ones are taken care of in Rhodes."

"I've already discussed this with Dr Karavolis and requested that I have the Caesarean here, Cathy. I know it's serious but he's going to make an exception in my case. Because I'm a trained nurse and I know the risks, I also know the qualifications Dr Karavolis has in surgery and

I'm sure I'll be safe in his hands. This hospital is equipped with everything required, including an excellent surgical team. The specialist I've been seeing over on Rhodes has also agreed to this because he knows just how desperately I want my twins to be born on my beloved island."

Cathy smiled as she secretly admired her patient's positive attitude to her condition. "In that case, I'll try to be with you at the birth."

"Thank you. I'd like that very much."

Sister Maria arrived back, saying she was going to take Ariadne for her scan.

Maria handed Cathy another set of case notes referring to the patient in the next cubicle. Cathy moved on, scanning the notes as she went. Tatiana, her next patient, was being treated by weekly injections of a new anti-miscarriage drug.

Before giving the injection Cathy asked her patient if she'd had any side effects.

Tatiana smiled. "Nothing at all to worry about. I was so pleased when the doctor suggested he would like to try this new drug. I've had three miscarriages and I'm so anxious not to lose this one."

After giving the injection, Cathy turned round to put the kidney dish back on her trolley.

Yannis was standing in the doorway, watching her. "How are you getting on?"

No smile, no sign that they were anything but medical colleagues. Exactly how it should be, Cathy thought, ignoring the confused feelings inside her.

"Fine!"

"I'd like to take you up to Theatre before I start on my list. I may not have time to show you around before I need you to assist me some time in the near future so I've told Sister Maria I'd like to take you away from Outpatients for a short time."

He moved into the cubicle and smiled down at the patient. "Looks like you're going to be fourth time lucky with this baby, Tatiana. I had a word with your obstetrician over on Rhodes after your last appointment there and he's very pleased with your progress."

Tatiana beamed up at the handsome doctor. "I won't have to go over to Rhodes for the birth, will I? I'd much prefer to be here."

"Unless some complication develops, there's no reason why you shouldn't be delivered here."

"My husband's already planning the celebration. You're invited, of course, Dr Yannis. You were the one who suggested I should go over to Rhodes and see this doctor who specialises in women who've miscarried. I understand that he's also a friend of yours."

"Yes, he was at medical school with me...a long time ago." Yannis swung round. "Must go. Take care of yourself and that precious baby, Tatiana."

Cathy increased her speed to keep in step with Yannis as they went down the corridor together. His face was solemn again, but she was glad she'd noticed the easy, friendly manner he adopted with the patients.

Tatiana had been obviously delighted to see him. Patients and staff alike seemed to regard him as a heart-throb, from what Tanya had told her before she'd gone off to Australia. But Yannis seemed totally oblivious to the effect he had on the opposite sex.

"I thought it would be a good idea for you to familiarise yourself with our operating theatres before you're called on to work there. I've checked up on your CV and found you've had considerable experience in surgery."

"Yes, I was fortunate to have a lot of experience in my early career. I toyed with the idea of specialising at one point but decided to gain wider experience so that I could possibly train as a GP after I'd settled down and had a family."

He turned to look down at Cathy, realising for the first time that he was walking too quickly—as often happened when he was nervous. And he was nervous now. Cathy had that effect on him. He'd no idea why—well, he had, but now wasn't a good time to dwell on it.

"So you always intended to settle down and have a family?" He slowed his pace to a halt so that he could take a proper look at the attractive woman beside him.

She smiled up at him, relieved that he'd called a halt. "I never actually made any firm decisions about anything in my early career. Things just sort of happened and I went along with the flow. I always wanted to be a doctor but...what kind?" She spread out her hands in front of him. "That changed as I went along, always becoming enthusiastic about the project I was on at the moment and..."

"That's good! To be enthusiastic about your job, I mean."

He couldn't help admiring the way her clear

blue eyes shone when she found a subject that interested her.

"Not unless you end up as a kind of jack of all trades, master of none."

"I think you underestimate your career progress so far," he said quietly as he decided he really should make the effort to move on.

"You've got a wealth of experience, which will come in useful in a hospital like ours. Here on the island we have a certain amount of autonomy. In emergencies we have to take decisions whether to operate on a dangerously ill patient or to have him or her transferred over to the bigger hospital in Rhodes. If time is against us or if, due to adverse weather conditions, the helicopter ambulance is grounded, we have to go ahead with the necessary surgery here."

A couple of nurses had just passed by, giving them inquisitive glances. He didn't want to give any cause for tongues to start wagging. "As far as I can see, you've steered a steady course since you qualified, gaining a great deal of valuable experience. And this was to achieve your aim to become a GP, you say?"

"I figured it would make sense if I were to find

my life partner and settle down to have a large family."

"Your life partner?" His brown eyes were searing into hers. She held her breath, mesmerised by being the centre of his attention. "Do you believe there is a designated person who is meant to be your life partner, your soul-mate?"

Oh, heavens! She wished she hadn't started opening up to him like this.

"Possibly," she said softly, her eyes searching his face. "At least, I did when I was much younger, before I became…disillusioned."

"Oh, you must never become disillusioned about love," he said in a husky, deeply sensual voice.

Looking down at Cathy now, he was trying hard to remind himself that he'd already experienced what it was like to have a soul-mate. His hand moved as if by someone else and gently touched her face, her skin so soft, her expression so vulnerable.

"You've just been unlucky," he finished off quietly. "But don't give up hope." He put his hand under her elbow. "We'd better get on. I'm expected to in Theatre shortly."

As they walked along together again, he was telling himself that he would like to see Cathy settled with a life partner. It would suit her. She was obviously a devoted and competent mother, running a career and parenthood at the same time with no help from a partner. He swallowed hard. How ironic it was that he'd lost his partner and his unborn child and here was a young woman with a child and no man to love her.

He was bound to Maroula even though she wasn't there. And Cathy, with her unfortunate, if mysterious, experiences in the past making her wary of forming another liaison certainly wouldn't want to take on a grieving widower.

They were reaching the surgical suite. He gave Cathy a whistle-stop tour of Theatre number three which he knew to be empty. It would be easier to look around without having staff members there.

She was nodding. "It's very well equipped!"

He smiled. "Oh, yes, we're equipped for general surgery and most specialist procedures."

A nurse pushed open one of the swing doors. "We're ready for you now, Dr Yannis."

"Is the anaesthetist here?"

"Yes, he's waiting for your instructions." She paused. "I'm afraid your assistant hasn't arrived yet. The morning boat from Rhodes is late due to the high wind that blew up during the night. Sister is trying to arrange for someone to take his place but—'

"Tell Sister not to worry. I'm sure Dr Meredith would assist me, wouldn't you?" He turned to Cathy. "They're well staffed in Outpatients this morning. You'd be more use up here in Theatre. What do you say?"

"If that's where you'd like me to work," she said evenly.

"Just for the first operation. It's an appendectomy so shouldn't take long. The patient has been having tests to check why she experiences occasional pain in the area of the appendix. After studying the results of the tests and scans, my conclusion is that it would be best to remove it. I put her first on the list and set the wheels in motion after you called in to see me this morning."

He turned to look at the young nurse. "You're sure our patient has been fully prepped? She's been starved long enough, hasn't she?"

"Yes, sir. She's had nothing to eat since midnight, hoping that you would decide to operate this morning."

"Excellent!"

Cathy scrubbed up at the next sink to Yannis.

She held her hands out. A nurse was waiting with a sterile gown to Velcro down her back. Gloves were peeled over her hands. Yannis glanced down approvingly. "Let's go."

She followed behind, noting that Theatre one was exactly like the one she'd just checked out. The surgical team looked alert and focused. Yannis raised an eyebrow above his mask as he looked across the inert figure towards Cathy.

"Scalpel, Cathy."

As she handed him the required instrument she was feeling relieved that he'd chosen to call her Cathy. He'd already introduced her as Dr Cathy Meredith to the assembled team. But it made her feel special, that she was some kind of friend with the surgeon. A kind of friend; that was a good description that she should try to remember if she could.

For the next half-hour she was totally committed to the task in hand. Yannis quickly cut through the patient's abdominal muscles to expose the angry-looking appendix. Yes, the patient would certainly feel much better when that infected organ was disposed of. Yannis was checking other organs in the vicinity.

"It's just the appendix that's infected," he told

the assembled team. "No other organ has been affected. Have the biopsies checked out, Sister. Let me know the results as soon as you get them back from the lab. I took a biopsy of this ovary as a precaution. It looks healthy enough but it's in very close proximity to the infected area."

The swing doors opened as a young, harassed-looking young man already swathed in surgical gown and mask arrived.

"Ah, Nikolas! Good of you to join us! Problem with the boat, I hear… Thank you, Cathy. You were a great help. You are free to go back to Outpatients now. I'll see you later."

Cathy smiled at the young man as she went out. From the greenish colour of his skin above the mask it looked as if he wasn't such a good sailor. "Sure you don't want me to take over for the morning, Nikolas?" she whispered as they passed each other.

"Better keep in with the boss," he muttered. "I'm new here and—"

"So am I." She pulled down her mask and smiled at the new recruit, who looked terrified of the ordeal ahead.

"When you've finished chatting, Nikolas,

you can bring the next patient in," Yannis said evenly.

Cathy turned to take a last look at the boss and was sure he winked at her over the top of his mask.

CHAPTER THREE

CATHY peeled off her surgical gloves and threw them into the bin before washing her hands. A couple of weeks had passed since she'd worked in surgery again with Yannis.

She'd been beginning to wonder if she'd done something he hadn't approved of on her first morning at the hospital. And then she'd remembered the wink he'd given her over the top of his mask as she'd been leaving Theatre one. Totally out of character! What had that been all about? Or maybe she'd imagined it. Yes, that was more like it. Because he'd given her precious little attention since then!

Oh, he'd called her into his office a couple of times but merely to brief her about a new patient or a different treatment that was going to be introduced. Off duty she hadn't seen him at all. Well, he did live near the sea and she was living in the upper town so there was really no reason why they should meet unless one of them arranged something socially. And it certainly wasn't going to be her! She understood the macho Greek mind too well from her holidays here on Ceres.

She'd felt nervous coming to the hospital this morning because Yannis had told her he'd scheduled her to work for the whole morning with him on his surgical list. She had been relieved to be asked, but apprehensive that she might do something to annoy him.

His manner had been totally professional and decidedly cool for the last few days and she had begun to think she'd misjudged the warmth he'd shown her on that first evening. So she was very relieved now that her morning's work in Theatre had gone well.

She glanced up at her reflection in the mirror above the sink in the ante-theatre.

Not a scrap of make-up. She didn't wear it when she knew she was needed in Theatre. In the mirror she saw the door opening as Yannis came in, shedding his theatre gown in the bin by the door.

He stood behind her. She watched his reflection as a broad grin came over his face. "Don't tell me. You were just about to put on your make-up and I've walked in so you don't want me to watch you. It's OK, I'll go out again."

She swung round. "No, you're OK. I wasn't going to put make-up on. Haven't got any with me."

"I'm glad."

He was standing very close. She could feel his hot breath on her face. He seemed to be studying her skin. She wondered if he'd noticed the spot that had developed on her right cheek.

"Yes, I'm really glad you've come into Theatre without make-up. It makes you look younger and I'm sure it's more hygienic."

"I've never worn makeup in Theatre." She was talking very quickly now, intensely aware of his close proximity. "Not since my professor of surgery at Middlefield General Hospital in Yorkshire ticked me off for wearing it. This particular professor claimed that make-up could harbour bacteria on the skin. He was probably right. And I'd found whenever I tried to wear make-up in Theatre it had gone all streaky anyway."

"It's an interesting theory. Turn round again. I'll help you out of your gown."

She put her hands in front of her defensively. "No, don't do that! I'm going to shower first in the female changing room. I…I'm not fully dressed underneath!"

"I wish you hadn't told me that," he said, his voice hoarse and seductively sexy.

He stepped back as he tried to get his hormones under control. He'd tried so hard for the last two weeks to keep control of himself. It was as if he was coming to life again. A wonderful feeling but he'd no idea how to handle it. Whenever he caught a glimpse of Cathy in hospital, walking down the corridor or bending over a patient, he felt like a teenager again.

He turned abruptly, the guilt of the confession he'd just made to himself rising up inside him alongside the disturbing sensations of sexuality and tenderness that he felt when Cathy was around. He'd forced himself to schedule her to assist him for the entire morning to prove that it was possible for him to remain totally professional.

And he had! But here he was, falling at the last hurdle. "Thanks for your help," he said evenly as he strode towards the swing door. He'd already pushed it open before the strong feelings she'd aroused in him became too much for him to ignore. He turned around again, letting the swing door close.

Cathy felt alarmed as she looked at his solemn face. He'd formally thanked her but was he now going to tick her off about the way she'd sutured that last patient? He'd been watching her so intently she was sure he was going to make some criticism.

"Cathy, I wonder if we could spend some time together this evening? I know we're both off duty."

He still wasn't smiling as he struggled to get his emotions under control.

Cathy had a surge of conflicting emotions herself at his suggestion. On the one hand her heart was telling her she'd love an evening out with this handsome Greek doctor. But her head was questioning whether that would that be wise. She had to be more careful than she had in the past. Meeting up casually with him on that first evening had been fun. But this invitation needed more thought.

She'd vowed not to go out with any man she was attracted to in case she made the same mistake she had in the past by falling for his charms only to be let down when she found out what he was really like. And, anyway, she shouldn't be mixing business with pleasure by going out with her boss. However would she manage to work with him if they started dating?

"Yannis, I hardly know you," she blurted out. "Don't you think it's a bit soon to have a date together?"

For a brief moment he looked perplexed before he managed to reply in a composed tone of voice. "I think you've misunderstood the situation, Cathy. I was merely wanting to have a chance for us to discuss how things are going for you here at the hospital in a less formal setting, away from work."

Oh, heavens! She'd put her foot in it again. How embarrassing to jump to conclusions like that! She felt crushed.

She hesitated before replying. His suggestion now seemed harmless enough. This was by no means an average type of man. Not the men she'd known in her life anyway!

"Well, yes, I agree it would be nice to have time to discuss things when we're not busy in hospital. What did you have in mind?"

Yannis was watching her reactions, trying to look composed but feeling utterly foolish for asking her out in the first place. Whatever had he been thinking? He was so rusty he had no idea how to talk to women any more!

Yes, what did he have in mind? If only he knew! He swallowed hard. "Would you like to come and have supper at my place?"

She hesitated once more. Having misinterpreted the situation completely, she knew she should make up for her faux pas. There would be no harm in simply chatting over supper.

She took a deep breath. "Yes, I would enjoy that. Thank you, Yannis," she said politely.

Relief flooded through him!

"Good! My housekeeper will be delighted if I do some entertaining for once. She's a very good cook but I don't give her enough practice. Most evenings I tell Eleni I don't need her so she goes home to her husband in Nimborio."

He was talking very quickly now, anxious to disguise his nervousness and get the preliminaries out of the way. "Oh, and do feel free to bring Rose along. All the taxi drivers know where I live now. About eight o' clock OK?"

"Fine!"

He left the room abruptly without a backward glance. Outside the door he paused for a couple of seconds to gather his breath. There! He'd taken the first step towards…towards what? Was he going in entirely the wrong direction? Would it all be a disaster? The emotional turmoil inside him didn't augur well. But he felt driven on by forces beyond his control. Was he betraying Maroula's memory by contemplating an evening in the company of another woman, someone he found very attractive and wanted to spend time with?

He sighed as he moved off down the corridor in the direction of his office. Only time would tell and at this moment he wished he could see into the future. Best to simply not look too far ahead. Only as far as this evening.

Cathy was as nervous as if she was going on her first date. She had to keep on reminding herself that this evening wasn't actually a date. She was simply going to her boss's house for supper and his housekeeper would be doing the cooking. It would be a treat to be spoiled like that—and nothing more!

Her face in the mirror certainly looked an improvement on the face that had stared back at her at the end of a morning in Theatre. And so it should after the time she'd spent covering up that

spot on her right cheek, blending in the founda-
tion with the light suntan she'd managed to get by
playing in the sunshine with Rose whenever she'd
had some off-duty time during the day. And she'd
changed the shade of her lipstick three times.

She put the third lipstick down. That was fine.
By the time she'd drunk a couple of glasses of
wine and swallowed a few olives, she'd have
licked it all off anyway. She stood up, adjusting
the waist tie on her white cotton top. Too much
cleavage?

If you've got it flaunt it, as her mother used
to say. But what did she know about relationships? She'd had almost as much bad luck as
her daughter! And Cathy was determined not to
flaunt herself tonight. She was intent on being
totally platonic with Yannis who obviously simply
wanted to be a friendly and concerned boss by
inviting her to supper. She readjusted her top so
that it was in no way provocative.

Her mobile rang. It was Anna. Her son, Manolis,
had presented her with a mobile phone before he'd
gone off to Australia. Cathy was glad she could
stay in contact with Anna throughout the day
when she was looking after Rose. This evening,
on hearing that Cathy had been invited out, Anna

had insisted it would be better for Rose to stay at her house and get a good night's sleep.

"I meant what I said earlier," Anna said now, shouting as she always did when she used her mobile. "Just enjoy yourself this evening, Cathy, and don't worry about Rose. She's already settled down in my children's dormitory room. I've got two of my granddaughters in there too, so when she wakes up she'll have company. I'll call you in the morning. OK?"

"Thanks, Anna. I really..."

But the line had gone dead. What a wonderful woman Anna was! She'd devoted her life to her family and now, at an age when she could have had some time to herself, she'd chosen to look after the next generation and the next.

After much persuasion from Manolis, Anna had allowed him to pay a young woman from the village to help her. Cathy had insisted on being responsible for the wages now that Anna took charge of Rose whenever necessary. She'd also made an arrangement with the bank to have a percentage of her hospital salary put directly into Anna's account.

Her phone rang again almost immediately. It was the taxi she'd ordered. Apparently the driver was waiting for her at the end of the street. She picked up the new clutch bag her mother had given her before she'd left for Ceres. It was just big enough to hold a few euros, a comb, a lipstick and a tissue.

As she started out down the rickety wooden staircase, being careful not to get her heels caught in the gaps between the wooden steps, she couldn't help feeling a sense of apprehension at the evening ahead of her.

Yannis was waiting for her in the drive of his imposing house. She held her breath as she looked up at the impressive façade.

"This is some ancestral pile you've got here!"

Yannis gave her a nervous smile as he reached out to take hold of her hand. "Rose not with you?"

Cathy thought he looked decidedly disappointed that she hadn't brought her.

"Anna was insistent that it would be better for Rose to be put to bed at her house tonight. I don't like to argue with an older and wiser mother and grandmother."

He was still holding her hand. He raised it to his lips briefly.

They stood in front of each other face to face on the firm gravel, both of them almost too apprehensive to continue with this nerve-racking encounter.

"There's nothing ancestral about the house, I'm afraid," Yannis said as he led her inside. "It was a complete ruin when I bought it and the owners were glad to get rid of it. It took a year to rebuild. I got a good builder who suggested ideas and between us we came up with this."

He spread his arms wide as they stood together in the large square entrance hall where the ceiling was the height of the house. Through the vast skylight that formed most of the ceiling Cathy could see the darkening sky, streaked with the crimson and gold of the spectacular sunset.

"It's beautiful! The enormous curved skylight reminds me of a cathedral dome. Much smaller, of course. But however did you…?" She broke off, unable to voice the embarrassing, intrusive question.

As if reading her mind, Yannis enlightened her.

"You're wondering how I could afford this on my hospital salary? Two years before I came back to Ceres, my mother died and left me the family house where I was born over on the other side of the island."

"I'd no idea you came from Ceres. I thought you were born in Athens."

"No, I went to Athens to study medicine. That's where I met Maroula."

He broke off, wishing he hadn't said that. Surely it was time to stop equating everything with his wife, especially when he was entertaining Cathy for the evening and tentatively planning to move on. He swallowed hard as he realised what he'd just admitted to himself. Was it true? Did he dare? How would he cope with the feelings of guilt that were already creeping up on him?

Cathy stared at her host for the evening. He appeared to have been suddenly struck dumb.

She put her hand on his arm. "Are you OK, Yannis? You look…"

He covered her hand with his own and flashed her a grateful smile. "Yes, I'm fine, thank you."

He bent his head and kissed her on the cheek. Surprised, she turned her head towards him and he kissed her on the lips. Mmm, that was better. He savoured the taste of her lips before gently pulling himself away and gazing down into her dazzling blue eyes. It was so long since he'd felt such strong attraction. If he was being wicked now then the buzz he was feeling at this moment was surely worth the agony of guilt that could possibly ensue.

Surprised but struggling to conceal her emotional turmoil, Cathy said, "You were telling me about your family house."

"Yes." He took hold of her hand and led her towards the kitchen at the back of the house. "The family house happened to be on prime land at a time when more and more tourists were taken with the idea of buying a holiday house on Ceres. I instructed my solicitor to sell it and that was how I was able to buy this ruin and turn it into the house I now have."

They were going into the kind of kitchen that would be described in English magazines as a farmhouse kitchen. Cathy looked around her in wonder.

Her feet positively danced across the stone-flagged floor towards the picture window overlooking the inlet of sea and the hills across the other side.

"It's superb! Did you design this, Yannis?"

"Partially," he conceded, wryly. "I had a lot of input from a friend of mine who's an architect. I met him when Maroula and I lived…in our house in Athens. I told him exactly what I wanted here. It's not so different from…from what we had in Athens."

A small plump lady bustled in through the open door that led to the garden. "Yannis, I've got the herbs you need to add to the soup. I'll put them in now so that they've got time to—"

"Eleni, this is Cathy, the new doctor from the hospital."

Cathy held out her hand towards Eleni, who reached forward and grasped it.

"Good to meet you, Doctor. I'm glad you're coming to keep Yannis company this evening. He spends too much time by himself. Not good. A man needs—"

"Thank you, Eleni. I'll put the herbs in if you want to get off now."

"Well, yes, I do. If I'd known you were going to need me this evening I wouldn't have arranged to look after my grandchildren. Normally, I—"

"Supper's in the oven so I'm fine, Eleni. Thank you for getting everything ready. I'll see you tomorrow. *Kali nichta.*"

"*Kali nichta*, Yannis, Cathy."

"Absolute treasure, that woman," Yannis said

as he moved across to open the fridge. "Would you like a glass of champagne, Cathy?"

"That would be lovely." She perched on the counter beside the oven. "What's in the oven?"

Yannis was holding the top of the bottle, waiting for the little fizz that would indicate the imminent popping of the cork. "I think Eleni said it was chicken…or it might have been lamb. I've got to take it out at eight-thirty and the vegetables are prepared and waiting to be cooked in the steamer."

"You're right. Eleni is a treasure."

He handed her a glass. "Don't I know it? Maroula was a good cook so…" He broke off. "*Yamas!* Cheers!"

Cathy took a good mouthful as she reflected that she somehow had known that Maroula would have been a good cook. Yannis had got a perfect kitchen. All it lacked was a perfect woman. Good thing she was intent on keeping a totally platonic friendship with Yannis. Her own cooking would never match up! She loved to mess about, throw things into a casserole and leave them to their own devices in the oven.

On the other hand, she could learn! But would

that be to impress Yannis? Of course not, she told herself firmly.

"Would you like me to take a look in the oven?" She put her glass down on the counter.

"That might be an idea. I'll put these herbs in the soup while you're doing that."

"I'll do it, Yannis." She picked up the plate and surveyed the green fronds. "Oregano, my favourite." Sprinkling it liberally into the simmering soup, she turned her attention to the other herb. She wasn't at all sure what it was but if Eleni had thought it OK for the dish, who was she to argue?

"What's that you're adding, Cathy?"

It came to her in a flash of desperation. "Rosemary. So I think we might be having lamb." Thank goodness she remembered something from watching her mother deal with the Sunday joint.

She surveyed the work surfaces. "Do you know where Eleni keeps her oven gloves? Ah, there they are." Peering into the oven, she could tell immediately by the mouth-watering smell that it was indeed a leg of lamb in the oven.

She lifted it out carefully and basted it with the juices. Yes, it was all coming back to her. Piece of cake this cooking lark, especially if somebody had prepared everything in advance!

She pulled herself to her full height again, hoping that Yannis had noticed how experienced she was. So she was trying to impress him! No, she was simply trying to help a friend who happened to be a man on his own.

"It's roasting nicely," she told him, as if she did this sort of thing every day. "I can see it's a leg of lamb. Eleni has chosen to slow roast it,which means it should be very tender and taste delicious. Yes, another fifteen minutes will be about right."

He put a hand in the small of her back as he guided her along towards the sitting room. She was immediately drawn to the wide picture windows that were thrown open, protected by a vast insect screen on the outside.

"The view from here is superb!" She sank down on the sofa by the window. Yannis joined her, setting the champagne bottle down on a nearby table.

They were both silent as they looked out across the stretch of water to the other side where the steep sides of the hill plunged into the depths.

"I swim every morning," he said quietly. "It's a good way to start the day."

"Did you…?" She stopped.

"Did I used to swim with Maroula when she was alive? No, she couldn't swim. I tried to teach her but she didn't take to it."

Cathy remained quiet. How had he known that was what she was going to ask? Was it because she felt all the time that they weren't really alone? There was always a third person with them. A perfect, unblemished woman who could do no wrong.

She shouldn't resent that. It was churlish of her to be so petty as to deny Yannis the pleasure of talking about his wonderful wife. If it helped in the healing process then she was glad to be of service.

She stood up and murmured that she would check on the lamb.

It looked fine when she lifted it out and placed it on the serving dish that had been prepared near the oven. Somewhere at the back of her mind she had a vision of her mother hovering over the Sunday joint.

She could hear her voice now. "You've always got to let lamb rest before you serve it," she'd said way back in those days when she'd introduced a new boyfriend to their small family of two people, her father having long ago deserted the domestic bliss that her mother so yearned to create.

The soup smelt delicious and was still simmering along, creating a mouth-watering aroma across the kitchen.

"Shall I set the table?" Cathy motioned towards the large wooden table in the middle of the kitchen.

"Eleni has set the dining-room table. I'll take the soup through." He picked up the soup pan and poured the contents into a tureen that Eleni had placed in a strategic position beside the cooker.

She followed Yannis into the dining room. This was another room with the wow factor everywhere. A crystal chandelier in the centre of the room illuminated the table perfectly and brought dancing lights out from the crystal glasses on the table. Yannis put the soup tureen down on the table and lit the central candelabrum before holding out a chair for her.

He sat down at the head of the table. Cathy was sitting beside him on his right side. He served the soup and watched her take her first taste.

She raised her eyes to his. "Delicious!"

"Eleni makes delicious soup with vegetables from the garden. Courgettes and…er…*melejanes.* How do you say that in English?"

"Aubergines." She took another sip from her spoon.

"Yes, aubergines, beans, carrots—in fact, whatever the gardener tells her is ready to be used."

"I love making soup," she said, surprising both of them.

"Do you?" He smiled. "Somehow, I can visualise you in Theatre but not working over a hot stove. When did you learn to cook?"

"I learned all the simple stuff like soup from my mother when I was a child. Later on she used to tell me to get on with my homework, because she just knew I was destined to be a doctor. So I had to work hard at my schoolwork because I needed scholarships or grants to pay for my expensive education. Money was always scarce at home. But I could easily get back into the swing of cooking again if…if I had to."

"I would imagine you've got enough to do working full time in hospital and looking after your daughter."

Don't underestimate me, she thought as she put

down her spoon. I may yet surprise both of us if these home-making vibes continue to grow.

They moved on to the next course. "This lamb is superb," he said. "I'm so glad you supervised it at the end. It made all the difference."

"Don't patronise me," she said, with a grin.

He smiled. "I would never patronise you, Cathy. You never fail to surprise me with your many skills."

He leaned across to pour some red wine from the bottle, which he'd just opened, into her glass.

At the end of the meal she managed to eat a small portion of the freshly baked apple tart so that Eleni wouldn't be disappointed with their fast-fading appetites.

"Let's take our coffee out to the veranda," Yannis said, standing behind her chair to help her as she stood up.

He guided her through the French windows at the end of the dining room to an insect-proof veranda with another moonlit view of the sea inlet at the end of the garden.

He went out to the kitchen, returning with a glass of Metaxas brandy, which he placed beside her tiny coffee cup. For a few minutes they sat quietly, simply soaking up the nocturnal sounds.

An owl hooted from somewhere on the dark side of the house. A gentle breeze was murmuring over the sea. She could almost sense the salty depths beneath it.

He was close beside her now. Alarm bells were ringing in her head. Was she letting down her guard? The trouble was it felt so right to be here together. She'd never enjoyed anything that could remotely have been called domestic bliss in the whole of her life. Neither had she ever seen her parents sitting together like this, simply enjoying each other's company. The little she remembered of her frequently absent father was that in the evenings he'd preferred to go out alone to the pub or whatever took his fancy. When she was four he'd gone out for the evening and never come back.

"You're looking very solemn." He moved closer until his thigh was almost touching hers.

"I was just thinking how nice it is to sit here, doing nothing. Simply listening, thinking, enjoying being with…being with someone you can get on with."

"It's a long time since…" He broke off. "Yes, I'm enjoying having you with me. It's good feeling that I can tell you things and you won't… well, like that first night when we were by the sea at Michaelis's taverna. I felt quite comfortable talking to you about Maroula. I've never told anyone before. It helped."

"I'm glad. I'd like to see you…getting over your loss."

He took a deep breath. "I haven't been entirely honest with you, Cathy. I've never been able to tell anyone exactly what happened the day that… the day that Maroula died."

She waited, feeling that if she spoke she would break the spell that seemed to have descended over them.

"Maroula had gone to stay with her parents for the weekend. It was her mother's birthday. I'd been invited as well, of course, but I was due to give a paper at an important medical conference on the Saturday. I was terribly ambitious in those days. My medical career took precedence—even over the needs of my family."

She could hear the stress in his voice. "Don't beat yourself up," she said gently.

He looked at her with wide staring eyes and the anguish she saw in them was heart-breaking.

"I said I would take a taxi out to her parents' house on the Sunday so that I could drive her back. But Maroula said the birthday celebrations would be over by then. She would drive back during the afternoon. I'm ashamed to say that I felt relieved that I didn't have to leave the hospital on that Sunday because I had ward rounds to make in the morning and preparations for the week ahead. I was in line for a consultant position and anxious to create a good impression."

He brought both his hands up in front of his face almost as if he was praying. She waited. When he took his hands away, he turned towards her again.

"At the back of my mind I was worried about the drive that Maroula had to do down winding roads from her parents' house in the country. She was nearly seven months pregnant."

"She was pregnant?" Cathy echoed softly, immediately wishing she'd kept quiet.

"Yes, you asked me last time we talked together if I'd had children with Maroula and I said it wasn't to be—or something like that." He hesitated. "Well, we were expecting our first child. Scans had proved we had a son on the way."

Cathy could feel the tears welling up behind her eyes. Should she tell him to stop now? She didn't want to know the details of how his wife and their unborn child…

"Maroula was making her way down from her parents' house on that fateful Sunday afternoon. It was raining heavily. The road dipped into a narrow ravine and then climbed steadily to the top before the final descent. I was told by a man who was in a car only metres behind her that a big lorry had come round the hairpin bend near the top on the wrong side of the road and ploughed straight into her. She stood no chance."

It was now so quiet she could hear the clock ticking. She daren't move or speak.

Yannis was sitting bolt upright staring in front of him, trying to deal with the confused emotions coursing throughout his whole body. He wanted to go on speaking until he'd told Cathy everything he knew.

It was almost as if he was talking to the priest in the confessional when he was a teenager. He had to keep going even though he wanted to give in to the tears that were threatening to make him stay silent again for ever, never to have told a living soul the hell he'd gone through, the guilt he carried with him.

"The police rang me at the hospital. They said an ambulance was bringing Maroula into the hospital. I was to stay put and wait for her. I went out to the ambulance. The paramedics had already covered her face with a sheet."

"Oh, no!" She pressed her hands against her lips to stifle the sobs that were welling up in her throat.

"Maroula had been killed outright and our baby with her. In that moment of impact I'd lost both of them."

CHAPTER FOUR

WHEN he'd finished speaking she couldn't stop her arms from reaching out towards him in a completely involuntary gesture. It was if they moved of their own accord regardless of the consequences.

He was drawn towards the expression of compassion in her eyes. As he tried to stifle the tears and then the sobs that choked in his throat, threatening to destroy all his macho credentials, he couldn't help moving into the warm, comforting embrace that, suddenly and bewilderingly, felt so right.

She held him against her as the tears rolled down her face. Listening to his heart-rending sobs only made her own tears increase. She wanted to take his anguish away from him but felt utterly powerless.

Suddenly he became quiet and pulled himself away.

"I'm sorry," he said, his voice hoarse with

emotion. "I haven't cried like that since I was a small child. It's not the sort of thing that men do, is it?"

Out of the corner of her eye she noticed some tissues on a nearby table. Gently, she eased herself up, trying not to dispel the undeniable feeling of closeness that now existed between them. Moving across the room, she took a couple of tissues for herself before handing him the box.

"Maybe you should have cried before," she said gently.

"I couldn't. I didn't even cry at the funeral. I've got used to keeping my emotions to myself. Just getting on with whatever life throws at me, I suppose."

He took a deep breath and, squaring his shoulders, he got up and moved towards the window, looking out across the water.

"I hope I haven't upset you tonight, Cathy."

She joined him at the window. "I feel honoured that you chose to tell me about…about the family you lost. I can see now why…"

"Oh, Cathy, you've been such a help tonight," he said, looking down at her, his eyes searching hers as he drew her into his arms.

She felt the vibrancy of his strong athletic body.

He was a magnificent, virile man. He shouldn't waste any more time living in the past. It was a wonderful gesture to honour the memory of his wife as he had done, but he needed to move on and start living in the present and for the future again. How could she persuade him that was the path to take? If only she could help him to do this.

But was it her place to try? What were her real motives? Was she being totally altruistic or did she have a vested interest in persuading him to start considering his own needs and the possibility of forming a relationship with...well, someone like herself?

Not with her previous disastrous experiences! She mustn't, simply mustn't get too involved.

He lowered his head and kissed her gently.

"Thank you for being here with me tonight. I feel...I feel for the first time I'm beginning to think about the future again."

She could feel his hard muscular body pressing against hers. In spite of the harrowing events he'd just described, she felt her own body yearning to respond to the nearness of him. But even as the realisation came she knew it wouldn't be appropriate so soon after they'd both shed tears for the two lives that had been taken away and the agony that Yannis had suffered.

She waited, hardly daring to speak as she watched him. Seconds passed before he took a deep breath and released her from his embrace.

"It's too late for you to get a taxi. And as Rose is safely tucked in at Anna's house, I suggest you stay here tonight," he said quietly. "It's been a harrowing end to our evening, hearing about the sadness in my life, so I'll take you to the guest room where you'll be comfortable. Early in the morning I'll drive you home."

He took her hand as they mounted the wide staircase together. The touch of his skin against hers was temptingly sexy. And going up the stairs with Yannis was making her think how wonderful it would be to spend a whole night with him. That's what she might have done in her previous life, before Dave had made her think hard before she gave in to romantic temptation.

He kissed her briefly at the door to the guest room before showing her inside, pressing a switch by the door that illuminated several beautifully shaded lights. Standing in the doorway, he made it quite clear that he was going to leave her alone.

"You'll find everything you need in here. Sleep well." He closed the door.

She heard the muted sound of his footsteps going away from her as she looked around the well-appointed room, the opulent, hand-made silk curtains, held back by swathes of tasselled, embroidered silken swathes. Taking off her shoes, she walked across the thick white carpet towards the bed, gently easing herself onto the white silk coverlet. She turned on her side and pulled the coverlet back to reveal white linen sheets. Nuzzling her face into the pillows, she allowed herself to imagine she wasn't alone.

And then she remembered Dave! The disaster that her affair had been. From meeting him in a Leeds wine bar on a girlie night out with a few friends when he'd singled her out. He'd asked her to have dinner with him the next evening.

He was so handsome, charming, attentive—and she'd fallen for his lies, taken him back to her flat after he'd wined and dined her the next evening, and they'd spent the most romantic night together. Shortly afterwards he'd moved in and they had been together for a whole year.

He'd told her his wife had left him and she'd comforted him—just as she had done with Yannis!

But Dave's story had been just that, a story. While she'd opened up her home and her heart to Dave, he'd been dividing his time between her and his wife and two children. He'd told her he hadn't any children—as Yannis had done on that first evening and had then told her later he'd lost a baby son! Oh, but she believed everything Yannis told her. He was not the sort of person who… Hang on! Should she trust her own terrible judgement on anything to do with men? She'd been far too gullible for far too long! Once bitten twice shy, and she'd been bitten more than once!

Dave had told her he was a banker in London when they'd first met. He'd come up to Leeds to see a client. After moving in, he used to stay in London Monday to Friday—at first! After a few months he began to have frequent business trips and sometimes she didn't see him for two or three weeks.

Shouldn't she have suspected something? The words *Love is blind* sprang to mind! Well, she'd certainly been blind to all his faults. In defence of her utter trust in him, she had also been busy working long hours in hospital so she hadn't had time to pine.

But she'd always found time to welcome him

back with open arms. She sighed. Much as she was attracted to Yannis now, she had to be careful not to get carried away. He was a good friend. They could have a platonic relationship. Yes, they could, couldn't they?

Neither of them was in a position to commit to a meaningful relationship. Apart from her fear of making another relationship mistake, there was Rose to consider. She mustn't put Rose through what her own mother put her through, bringing men into their lives, only for them to be gone before she knew it.

Her priority was her daughter. She must create and maintain stability for Rose. But that didn't mean she couldn't be Yannis's friend, of course. They could help each other emotionally. Yes, that was how she would deal with the situation, she told herself sternly.

Yannis went into his bathroom, stripped off and went into the shower. The water cascaded over his body as he tried to blot out the new sensations he'd had to contend with all evening. What was happening to him? It was as if he'd become two different people now. Half of him wanted to move forward as a free man who could make new, radical decisions about the future without reference to the past. The other half wanted to stay firmly rooted in the past with Maroula, which he'd felt was his duty since her life had been cut short. She'd had no chance of achieving her allotted lifespan.

But here he was, in good health, with a good career, and had now met a wonderful woman. Cathy made him feel so alive!

He stepped out of the shower and grabbed a towel from the freshly laundered pile near to hand. As he walked naked back into his bedroom he felt the urge to make love with Cathy. It had been so long since he'd felt like this, his body vibrantly pulsating, longing to give all he had and to be welcomed into the paradise of two bodies delighting in sharing themselves with each other.

He'd had several girlfriends before he'd met Maroula but he'd known almost at once that she was the one. The special woman he wanted to be with for the rest of his life. And he'd been completely faithful to her during their marriage and after her death.

He stretched himself out on the bed. But now there was Cathy. This whirlwind who'd come into his life, disrupting all his ideas of how he should conduct himself since he'd chosen to remain a confirmed bachelor. What was it about Cathy that made him think she could replace Maroula? When Maroula had died he'd decided that nobody should replace her. Maroula had been unique. No one could hold a candle to her.

But Cathy was also unique. She was a wonderful, compassionate, sexy, attractive woman and she was only a short distance away down the landing. He sat up. Should he…?

No, he mustn't give in! It was too soon. He must control himself until he felt absolutely sure that he could handle the feelings of guilt that would undoubtedly follow if he were to consummate his desires. He mustn't let his heart rule his head tonight.

Cathy awoke with the dawn sun streaming through the open casement window. The first sound that alerted her to the unfamiliar surroundings was the gentle lapping of the sea on the pebbled shoreline beyond the garden. She stepped out of bed onto the thick carpet, which tickled her toes and muffled the sound of her feet as she moved towards the open window.

She sat down on the cushioned window seat and leaned out, smelling the delicious scent of the frangipani still covered in early dew. Across the stretch of the narrow seawater inlet she could see the steep hillside rising up to be warmed by the sun's rays at the top. She'd always loved this early part of the day when everything was calm and unspoilt. She wouldn't think about the events of last night, the confused thoughts that had kept her awake.

The quiet knock on her door brought her back to reality. The day had begun and she could no longer live in dreamland.

"Come in," she said breathlessly.

"Did you sleep well?" He was standing on the threshold, his mid-thigh-length towelling robe drawn tightly around him, knotted securely round his waist.

"Yes," she lied. "Did you?"

He nodded, not wishing her to know the wicked thoughts that had plagued him all night, the number of times when he'd almost broken his resolutions.

"Come down when you're ready and we'll have breakfast."

"Actually, I ought to get back in case Rose wakes up early and Anna phones me."

"Yes, you must be there for Rose. Such a lovely little girl. You're very lucky to have her," he said, unable to disguise his wistful tone. "I'll drive you home as soon as you're ready."

"Give me five minutes. I'll shower when I get back, then I can change into my day clothes for the hospital."

As Yannis drove her up the side of the hill that led to Chorio, she looked out at the tiny boats bobbing in the water of the harbour. The higher they rose, the smaller the boats seemed to be.

"That's always fascinated me," she said. "The way boats and cars appear to be like little toys the higher you go."

He took one hand from the wheel and placed it on her thigh. "That's one of the things I like about you, Cathy. Your delight in simple things. Maroula was like that."

She could feel herself stiffen up as she heard him speaking his wife's name again. Was Maroula always going to be there with them? Would they ever be able to get away from this iconic woman?

Just as soon as the thought entered her head she chastised herself sternly. Why was she thinking of them as a couple when she'd vowed to herself that they were to be just good friends? And why did she suffer attacks of jealousy whenever Yannis mentioned Maroula's name?

He removed his hand and put it back on the wheel, sensing that he'd somehow offended her. It was difficult to understand women. He hadn't had enough practice recently. Last night she'd listened so intently to everything he'd told her about Maroula but this morning she seemed different.

They reached the end of the street just as her mobile started to shrill. Yannis switched off the engine.

"Yes, Anna?"

"Hope I didn't wake you up, Cathy. Rose is awake and keeps looking for you. Shall I…?"

"I'll come and get her now so she doesn't disturb your granddaughters…Yes, I'm already dressed."

She turned to look at Yannis. She remembered his wistful tone when he'd told her this morning how lucky she was to have Rose. On impulse she asked if he'd like to come in and have breakfast with them. "You were saying you'd like to see Rose again."

He smiled. "I'd enjoy that very much."

She handed him her keys. "Go inside and make yourself at home. I'll go and get Rose."

He was walking around the kitchen when she arrived with Rose in her arms, still swathed in the blanket Anna had insisted she needed in the early morning air.

His face lit up. "Oh, little Rose is so beautiful!"

"Would you like to hold her while I get breakfast?"

"Of course!" He held out his arms.

Rose turned to look up at her mother questioningly.

"It's OK, darling. Go to Yannis."

Rose turned her head and smiled at him.

She held out her arms towards his hair, suddenly remembering what fun it had been when she'd twirled it in her fingers.

As he took the child in his arms Yannis felt something akin to comfort flooding through him. This little trusting angel seemed to have been sent to take the place of… No, he mustn't think like that. This was Cathy's child. A completely different child from the son he'd lost. But the rush of paternal instinct that came over him was a wonderful experience.

Cathy turned round after switching the kettle on. What a touching picture. The obviously besotted Yannis holding her daughter as if she were a prize he'd just been awarded. She tried to obliterate the flights of fancy that were hovering in her head as she saw how easily Yannis interacted with Rose. For a brief second she allowed herself to imagine how wonderful it would if Yannis became part of their little family.

She gave herself a mental shake. The idea had to stay in fantasy land if she was to keep her resolutions intact.

"I'll get Rose dressed after breakfast but for the moment she can crawl over the floor if you watch her. I'll be putting her in clean pyjamas tonight so she can get as dirty as she likes—and she does enjoy getting dirty."

Yannis grinned. "So I see." He was following Rose as she made her way to the veranda. "It's OK, Cathy, I won't let her fall over the edge into the garden. Don't you think it would be a good idea to put a fence round the veranda now that she's moving so quickly? Would you like me to send someone up to do it today?"

She was putting yesterday's bread rolls under the grill. "That would be great if you could arrange it. I was planning to find a carpenter myself."

He picked up Rose from the floor and came over to stand behind Cathy.

She was acutely aware of him. He'd put after-shave on. She'd enjoyed breathing in the heady aroma as they'd come up the hill in the car but now, having him so close, it was putting her completely off what she was supposed to be doing. Good thing she wasn't in the operating theatre with him! It didn't matter if she burnt the rolls.

She swung round so that she was facing him, breathing in the combination of his natural male scent mixed with the one that came from a bottle.

"Would you really be able to organise the fence for today? I mean…"

He leaned even closer, his sexy lips curving into the most disarming smile that displayed his strong white teeth. His brown eyes were warm, compassionate and fixed on hers as if she was the only person in the world who mattered to him.

Gently, he touched the tip of her nose with

a teasing kiss. "Consider the job done." Rose, enjoying the warmth of what felt like a cuddle, reached out her hand and grabbed Cathy's hair.

"OK, Rose, I'll take you... Oh, bother! Yannis, you keep her for a moment while I try to salvage these bread rolls."

Yannis, holding onto Rose with one hand, switched off the grill. "I've got a better idea. Why don't I go to the bakery for some freshly baked ones?"

Minutes later they were sitting at the table out on the veranda, Rose strapped into her high chair, eating fresh rolls liberally covered in Anna's home-made plum jam.

Yannis picked up the cafetière and poured more coffee into Cathy's cup before refilling his own. "Rose looks as if she's enjoying herself."

Cathy smiled as she looked at her daughter, who was running her jammy fingers through her blond hair while she chewed.

"Who will you get to make a fence around the veranda?"

"Petros, Eleni's husband, who does the garden and takes care of all the house maintenance. He can turn his hand to anything, so a small fence won't be a problem. I phoned him while I was waiting to be served at the bakery. He'll be here soon to assess what he needs for the job."

"Such efficiency, Doctor!"

"Not really. I get spoiled in my domestic situation by Eleni and Petros. Nothing is too much trouble. They know I'm a widower and it's almost as if they're sorry for me being all alone. Do you know what I mean?"

She nodded as she swallowed a piece of roll. Oh, yes, she knew perfectly well what he meant but she wished she didn't have to be constantly reminded of his situation. She looked out across the garden towards the bay of Pedi at the bottom of the hill. Even though the sun was shining on the water and the sky was blue she felt as if a cloud had emerged, threatening her so far idyllic day.

"I'd better get Rose cleaned up and ready for me to take her back to Anna's when I go down to the hospital."

"You seem very comfortable here. This is Tanya's house, I believe?"

"Yes, she inherited it from her grandmother Katerina, who was a dear friend of Anna. Manolis was living in the house next door so when they got married they had a door knocked through—see it there at the side of the kitchen? I've got the key for that house as well but I prefer to stay in this smaller one."

"I remember Tanya telling me about it before she and Manolis went off to Australia. Manolis's house is called Agapi, which means love, doesn't it?"

"Yes, and this house is called Irini, which means peace," she said quietly. "Tanya told me that when she first started working in the hospital with Manolis she couldn't imagine how they could live next door to each other in houses called love and peace. They'd had a previous relationship with each other that hadn't worked out."

He reached across the table and covered her hand with his own. "You have an English saying that the path of true love never runs smoothly. It was certainly true in their case, I believe."

As she looked across into his eyes she wished the turmoil of her emotions would go away. Yannis was a true romantic. She shouldn't allow herself to dwell on the expression in his eyes when...

Rose was whinging, struggling to pull herself out of the straps in her high chair.

"OK, Rose, you've made your point." Cathy stood up briskly and released the straps, gathering up the sticky child into her arms. "We're heading for the bathroom now so if Petros arrives…"

"I'll get him started then I'll go to the hospital. He's bringing the replacement pushchair I had sent over from Rhodes. Petros said the old one you'd borrowed from Anna wasn't worth repairing so I've got a new one."

"That's very kind of you but…"

"I kept meaning to explain what was happening." He stood up, brushing a hand over his trousers.

"I think you've got some dirty marks from playing with Rose, Yannis. I'll get the clothes brush."

"No need. I've got spare clothes down in my shower room. Sometimes when I have a few hours off duty I go out in the boat and come back needing to change."

"You've got a boat?"

"Every man on Ceres likes to have his own boat! It's part of our Greek heritage. You must let me take you out in it when we're both off duty."

* * *

Walking down the *Kali Strata* some time later she was alarmed at the high wind that had started to whip up the waves down in the harbour. Further out to sea she could see the white caps on the waves. Men were pulling their boats out of the water up onto the side of the harbour. She knew this was a sure sign that a bad storm was on the way. As a child she remembered being marooned on Ceres for several days. During a bad storm the port authorities forbade any boats to leave or enter the harbour.

She quickened her step, anxious to get inside before the storm arrived.

As she walked into the hospital she was thinking she must make the effort to behave naturally when she met Yannis. The events of yesterday evening and the warmth she'd felt flowing between them this morning had bowled her over. She felt so different from the way she'd felt this time yesterday.

"Dr Meredith!"

Cathy walked briskly across to the reception desk. "Dr Karavolis is asking for you in Casualty. There's been a traffic accident."

"Thank you." As she hurried along the corridor she wondered how serious the accident could be. It seemed strange that traffic accidents could happen on this small island which, until recent times, had only had donkey paths. But traffic was building up now that more and more paved roads were being made. Many of the older roads tended to be too narrow for cars to pass each other. She hurried into the treatment room.

"Good. You're here!"

She didn't know if Yannis's peremptory tone had something to do with the fact that she'd taken too long getting down there.

"Take over from me, please. I've put it in the notes. Mario had this sedative…" he pointed to the notes "…five minutes ago so you can go ahead with fixing the cast. X-rays up there on the wall screen show the scaphoid bone is fractured. They're waiting for me in Theatre where two more of the accident patients require immediate attention."

The middle-aged man on the couch looked up at her beseechingly as Yannis swept out of the treatment room.

"Are you a proper doctor, miss?" he asked in Greek.

She smiled down at him and replied in the same language. "Of course I am. They wouldn't let me loose on you if I wasn't. I'm Dr Meredith from England, but you can call me Cathy."

"It's only that you look so young. I thought perhaps you were a student."

"Bless you! I'm thirty-one but don't tell anybody. Now, let me help you to sit up, carefully, slowly, yes, that's fine. I want you to hold this wooden roll in your hand for me. Now, I'm just going to bring your hand back a little so that the wrist will be in the correct position for the next six weeks."

"Six weeks? I've got a plumbing business to run, miss, sorry, Dr Cathy."

"Have you got an assistant?" she asked as she wound the bandage around his hand and up over the wrist.

"I've got two—my two sons. Twenty and eighteen."

"Well, as long as you give them the heavy work to do and you just supervise, you'll be OK. Once I've set this it will be good physiotherapy for you to keep the fingers moving. There! That's perfect!"

"How can you be so sure?"

She paused for a few moments to check the angle at which she'd set the fractured scaphoid.

"Well, the scaphoid bone is a tricky wrist bone. I've known one or two patients come into the hospital where I was working back home in England with complications usually caused by the wrist bones being set at the wrong angle. But I don't think that will happen in your case."

"Why?"

"You can never be sure of anything in orthopaedics. We're all at the mercy of the bone structure we started out with as children and the problems it's been subjected to over the years. Doctors apply their expertise but it's Mother Nature who has the last word."

"Thanks, Cathy. You've been great. Can I go now?"

"Is anybody with you?"

"Not yet. My wife's gone over to Panormitis to see her mother. She won't be back till this evening. I phoned my sons and they're coming as soon as they've finished putting in the shower rooms at the new hotel. I told them I was OK, just a broken wrist or something. I told them not to leave the job until they'd finished. I can't afford to lose the contract I've got with the hotel. I said I'd phone them when I'd been seen by a doctor."

"What actually happened?"

Outside the treatment room she could hear voices and people moving around. She would have to take on some of the work as soon as she'd finished with Mario.

Her patient frowned as he tried to remember the details of the crash. "I was coming down the hill from Chorio in my lorry, having dropped off my boys at the new hotel. Everything was OK until I reached the corner at the bottom of the hill. The bus loaded with passengers was coming along from the harbour at its usual steady pace when a man in a flash sports car behind me, who'd already hooted at me twice, overtook on the bend."

Cathy put her hand over her mouth. "Oh, no! Not on that narrow bend by the water."

"Exactly so! Well, the bus swerved and demolished the side of the house alongside as the driver slammed on his brakes. The sports car went straight into the water, after he'd clipped the side of my cab and thrown me against the dashboard with my arm outstretched."

"So what happened to the sports car driver?"

"Hopefully he's in hospital here. The last thing I saw as they carted me off in the ambulance was a couple of policemen diving into the water, trying to find him. A crane had arrived to fish out the car. The ambulance was having to do several trips, I believe, because of all the stretchers from the bus."

She could feel the hairs on the back of her neck standing up in horror. However many times she had to attend the aftermath of a serious crash she still couldn't keep herself from feeling shocked. No wonder Yannis had been abrupt with her when she'd arrived.

"Are you OK to call your sons and tell them what's happening or shall I do it?"

"I'm OK. It's only my left arm." He was already fishing in his pocket for his mobile.

"Tell them you're going to rest here until they come for you this evening. I'll find you a bed or a quiet corner." She took a peek outside the treatment room. Hopefully! She called a nearby nurse and asked her to see that Mario was taken care of till his sons arrived.

"Come back to Outpatients in a week's time and ask to see me, Mario."

Her patient smiled. "I'll look forward to that, Cathy."

Another patient was wheeled into the treatment room on a stretcher as Mario was taken away in a wheelchair.

CHAPTER FIVE

"You need to take a break, Yannis," Cathy said gently.

They were both in the anteroom of the theatre, Yannis still in his theatre gown, leaning against the sink as he studied the tail end of the list of the RTA patients who still needed to be dealt with.

"At least we haven't had any fatalities," he said, without looking up from the list. "In another couple of hours I reckon we should have everything under control."

"Yannis." She spoke a little louder. "You have two excellent young surgeons in there, part of a team who've just come on duty. Let them take over where we've left off. I'm exhausted."

"Cathy, I'm not suggesting you stay on any longer." He crossed the room and stood looking down at her in concern. "You've been assisting me since midmorning and it's now…" He stared up at the clock. "I hadn't realised it was so late."

"Exactly! I'm not going off duty unless you

do. You're exhausted but you won't admit it. You've got to delegate these two final operations to your staff. You need to rest now so that you'll be fit to deal with all our post-operative patients tomorrow."

He stared at her. Nobody had spoken to him like that for a long time. Maroula had always tried to make him take more care of himself. Was it possible that Cathy really cared for him? Just like Maroula had?

"OK. You're probably right," he said quietly. A wry grin spread across his face. "I'll go and do some delegating. And you must go off duty. Will you come along to my office when you're ready to leave the hospital?"

He gave her no time to answer as he disappeared through the swing doors back into Theatre.

She pushed open the door into the corridor and made her way down to the female medical staff changing and shower room.

"I'm ready to go home now." She stood in the doorway of Yannis's office. He was holding open the door, already looking more refreshed than he had done in the theatre anteroom. She noticed his dark hair still wet from the shower, his casual clothes—jeans and a T-shirt. Nobody seeing him now would think he'd been working all day in Theatre, in some cases saving lives.

She'd made the effort to improve her appearance. But it would take more than showering and putting on the clothes that had been stuffed in her locker since she'd donned theatre greens hours earlier to make her feel presentable. Still, she only had to get herself up the *Kali Strata* and home again where she could relax and look as scruffy as she liked.

Thank goodness the storm had abated for the moment. She'd been aware of the rain lashing on the windows, the wind whistling round the hospital while she'd worked. The helicopter ambulance was grounded and no boats were allowed into or out of the harbour, which had meant they hadn't been able to offload the more serious patients and make their workload easier.

He put a hand on her arm. "Quick drink? Down at the harbour? The rain's stopped now and the wind has died down. I presume you've been in touch with Anna about looking after Rose longer than expected?"

"I phoned this afternoon to tell her about the emergency situation. She'd heard all about it.

News travels fast on Ceres. She was already planning to take care of Rose until tomorrow morning. Told me to get a good night's rest when I came off duty. So I'm going to get back home, Yannis. It would be lovely to collect Rose if she's still awake—"

He put a hand on the small of her back. "Well, you need a little relaxation first, Doctor, then I'll put you in a taxi and send you up the hill to your bed."

Yannis was probably right. She did need to unwind first. It had been an exhausting day.

"OK. But just one drink and then…"

"Yes, yes, I understand, Cathy."

It was good to feel she was being taken care of as he steered her along the corridor. This was something she hadn't felt with any of the men in her life. The emphasis they had insisted on had usually been pleasure, having a good time and, of course, sex. As long as they had been happy, that had seemed to be all that mattered to them. Consideration and caring didn't come into it and she'd got used to thinking that was the norm. Especially after witnessing the way her father had treated her mother.

As they went out through the side door of the

hospital into the still warm night she was think-ing that this caring attitude was a two-way affair. She'd felt the need to protect Yannis and make sure he didn't tire himself out. Had she ever cared enough for any man to worry like that before?

They were walking side by side down to the harbour now. His hand was hanging loosely by his side and she knew he wouldn't try to hold hers. Not here in downtown Ceres where it would be noticed and gossiped about. They were simply good friends and colleagues relaxing after a hard day.

He chose a table right by the waterside. The plastic chairs were still wet from the rain. A young waiter came out with a cloth and wiped the seats.

"Just look at the white caps out there on the top of the waves," Yannis said, pointing out to the rough sea while the waiter dealt with the water on their chairs and table. "The port authorities were predicting on the radio just now that no boats would sail tomorrow. And the helicopter ambu-lance isn't allowed to fly either, because the wind may soon start again. It's going to be impossible to transfer any of our patients to Rhodes."

"Oh, well, we're coping OK, don't you think, Yannis?"

He smiled down at her. "We've got a good team at the hospital."

She sat down and ran a hand through her hair. It felt such a mess. She hadn't had time to dry it properly after her shower and it was going all curly.

He put a hand across and touched a strand of hair where it fell onto her shoulders.

"Leave your hair casual like it is now. Looking across the operating table when we'd finished this evening, I thought what a pity it was you had to keep your gorgeous hair locked up under your theatre cap all day."

"It doesn't feel very gorgeous now."

"Believe me, it is." He moved his hand up, allowing his fingers to run through the freshly washed, scented hair before leaning back against his chair where he had a perfect view of this wonderful woman who was bringing him to life again.

A waiter arrived at their table so he ordered a bottle of wine and some mezes. He looked across the table to see if Cathy was in agreement.

She hesitated, wondering how long this was going to take. But she realised she was ravenously hungry. "Probably a good idea to eat something. I haven't had anything to eat since breakfast, have you?"

Yannis shook his head. "Never even thought about it. Food and drink is what you need to help you unwind. I can see you're as tense as a coiled spring."

"Is that your diagnosis, Dr Karavolis?"

"Yes, it certainly is!" He signalled the waiter back and gave their order.

They sat without speaking for a while, simply soaking up the after-work atmosphere by the water's edge. Snippets of Greek conversation could be distinctly heard around them.

"Terrible crash!"

"They got the driver of the sports car out of the harbour."

"Well, of course they'll charge him with dangerous driving!"

"Terrible injuries."

"In the hospital, of course."

Yannis leaned across the table. "It seems everybody knows more about what's happening than we do!"

She smiled and leaned closer so that their heads

were almost touching. "We merely patch people up."

"*Signomi, ghiatro.* Excuse me, Doctor, but I just wanted to say thank you for taking care of my husband today."

Cathy looked up at the pleasantly plump middle-aged woman who was standing by her chair. By the woman's side was her patient Mario, sporting his new cast, which was already covered in signatures, looking slightly embarrassed that his wife had insisted on approaching the doctor while she was off duty and trying to relax.

"Mario told me how brilliant you were with him this morning. I can't thank you enough. And you, Dr Karavolis, you must have been working all day as well. We're all talking about the crash down here. Must have been terrible for you at the hospital."

"We're trained for that sort of thing," Yannis said quietly. "I'm glad Dr Cathy was able to help Mario."

Cathy could see that Mario was trying to pull his wife away from the two doctors. After the day they must have had the last thing they needed was a patient's relative bothering them.

"See you next week, Dr Cathy," he said cheerily, as he escorted his wife back to their table.

Yannis looked across at Cathy. "Maybe it was a mistake to come and sit outside such a crowded taverna."

"Not at all! It's good to join in sometimes."

"Meaning I usually prefer to spend my off-duty time by myself?"

"Well, I'm sure you weren't always like that. You've had a difficult few years and now it's time to come out of the hard shell you've built around yourself."

She picked up the glass of wine he'd just poured for her and raised it to her lips.

They began to eat from the plates of delicious mezes, olives, feta cheese, Greek salad, taramasalata, whilst chatting companiably to each other.

"I'm feeling a lot stronger now," she said as she put down her fork. "Hadn't realised just how hungry I was."

He reached across the table to take hold of her hand.

"Cathy, I can feel myself coming to life again. You're right. I had built a shell around me. Maybe it is time to move on. But...the trouble is there's always something inside me that holds me back. I feel guilty to be enjoying myself when..."

She waited, knowing he was thinking about Maroula but didn't want to say it out loud. Somehow he had to realise it was OK to feel as he did. But again she reminded herself it was Yannis's problem, not hers.

She put down her half-finished glass. She was physically exhausted and knew she couldn't deal with emotional problems tonight, her own or Yannis's.

"I'd like to get back home now before it's too late to get a taxi."

"You must be exhausted so that's probably a good idea," he said, standing up and signalling to the waiter. "There's a taxi coming along the quayside now. I'll get it for you."

Lying in her bed later, she looked out through the moonlit casement. Yes, it was going to be difficult to deal with the emotional problems ahead of her. She had to maintain a platonic relationship with Yannis but it was getting harder every time she was with him. But she had a history of giving her heart away too easily. She must keep on reminding herself that she wasn't going to have another meaningful relationship. Otherwise she would fall into the same trap she had with Dave. He'd had a real living wife always in the background.

She hadn't known about it otherwise she wouldn't have entered into a relationship with him. Yannis had put all his cards on the table. She knew the score, knew what she would be letting herself in for if she didn't stick to her resolutions. This time the wife would always be with them as a much-loved memory. Someone it would be difficult to live up to.

Did she want to put herself through all that? Again? Did she have the emotional strength in her? No, she didn't! No, a thousand times, no! Her head was telling her it would all end in tears again. But her heart was whispering it would be fun to have a romance with him. The trouble was she could feel herself falling for him. And it was so difficult to keep to her resolution not to.

But if she went along with her feelings it would be history repeating itself all over again. She should stay resolved that they were good friends only. They enjoyed being together.

A cloud was crossing over the moon. Was that

an omen? She closed her eyes so that she couldn't see it. Sleep would come eventually if she tried to stop thinking...

Yannis was standing on the balcony outside his bedroom, looking across the water at the moon above the hillside on the opposite side of the inlet. His thoughts were all about Cathy tonight, not Maroula, he realised. Since he'd moved into this house he'd found himself out here on so many nights in just this position. It was still the same moon that had somehow soothed him as he thought about Maroula. So why was he now thinking about Cathy? Was she beginning to take Maroula's place in his affections?

He gripped the rail that ran round the balcony. He still loved Maroula but he had deep feelings for Cathy. How did she feel about him? How could he find out unless he became closer to her?

He was longing to become closer to Cathy. Tonight as they'd sat beside the water in that crowded area of the harbour he'd longed to take her away, to be alone with her, just the two of them. But could he bear the feelings of guilt at his betrayal?

He had to take things slowly—for both their

sakes. He had to make absolutely certain that he could be with another woman whilst at the same time revering Maroula's memory. Cathy was too precious to have him toy with her affections only to decide he couldn't bear the guilt. For the moment he should simply enjoy being with her.

There was a big cloud occluding the moon now. He shivered as he turned to go inside.

A month later, as Cathy walked down the *Kali Strata*, she realised that the shock waves of the disastrous RTA were still being felt on the island. It had been the main topic of conversation everywhere she'd gone and had affected many lives. In the hospital they'd been extremely busy with inpatients and outpatients. But the main effect on her own life had been that she and Yannis had found very little time to relax together in an off-duty situation.

They'd both been working longer hours on duty. Yannis seemed to be taking his position as temporary director very seriously. When they'd seen each other briefly, usually at the end of the day, it had seemed that they were both treating each other warily.

As she reached the harbour-side she increased her pace. Yannis had sent her a text late last night asking her to meet him in his office early this morning.

When she arrived he opened the door and led her inside, suggesting they should sit in the armchairs over by the window. There was a cafetière of coffee and two cups on the small table.

"This all looks very civilised, Yannis. Not the way I usually start my day in hospital."

She sank down into one of the armchairs and allowed him to pour her a cup of coffee.

"So what are we celebrating?"

He smiled as he put down the cafetière. "I wanted to say thank you for all the extra hard work you've done over the past month and to tell you that we're resuming normal working hours from now on."

"Wow! That's good news!" She took a sip of her coffee. "So, what have you done? Sent all the patients home?"

"The majority of the RTA patients have now been discharged. I had to take on extra temporary staff and we've now reached the stage where we've got a good ratio of staff to patients. The patients with limb fractures still attend our orthopaedic clinics. All in all, I feel we've weathered the storm and we're steering in calmer waters now."

She smiled. "Talking of steering in calmer waters, have you been able to spend any time on that boat you were telling me you had? It must be very therapeutic to go out there on the sea."

He stared at her. Had she been reading his mind about the proposition he was about to put to her? But he had to tread carefully, not simply blurt it out.

"I'm afraid I simply haven't had time. It's still tied up to the jetty at the bottom of my garden. Petros checks it over and even goes out fishing on occasions, always bringing me back something for Eleni to cook for my supper."

He hesitated. "Eleni was asking about you the other day. Wondering when you were going to come round again. I told her we'd both been too busy."

She waited, hardly daring to breathe in case she broke the fragile ambience that was developing once more between them. It was true that during the past month they'd both been frantically busy. But on the rare occasions when they'd got together for a drink at the end of the day she'd felt he was decidedly wary with her.

Something seemed to have changed him since the night they'd had a drink down by the harbour and he'd told her he felt he was coming alive again. Perhaps he'd decided he preferred to stay with the past, to continue to worship at the altar of the iconic Maroula. In that case, she'd had a lucky escape that it was all going to end before she'd made a fool of herself-again!

She put down her coffee cup and stood up. "Thanks for the coffee. There's a patient I need to see before—"

"Cathy!" He moved swiftly to detain her. She hadn't given him time to work out what he was going to say even though he'd been thinking about it for days, ever since the workload in hospital had begun to ease off.

"I've made arrangements for us both to take the weekend off. I wondered if you'd like to go out in the boat with me?"

It had all come out in a breathless rush. Now all he had to do was hope she wouldn't come up with an excuse. After the busy month they'd both had he wouldn't blame her.

She stared at him. How could he suggest such

a thing? Just when she was beginning to reach a state of contentment in their seemingly platonic relationship! To be thrown together with him in his boat, spending the whole day in close contact? No, she mustn't! She didn't trust herself to stay focused on keeping her distance. If he made any kind of advances towards her... On the other hand, it would be wonderful to get out on the sea...and she could be careful not to get any silly romantic ideas. She'd been cooped up working in hospital for so long...

"Well, I'll have to check with Anna to see if she can look after Rose," she said carefully, playing for time to get her thoughts together.

"Oh, Rose is invited too, of course. I've really missed seeing her. We'd better get her kitted out in a small life jacket which she can wear when we're actually sailing."

Cathy could feel her interest in the idea increasing. If Rose was with them it would be OK, wouldn't it?

"The sea air would be good for Rose," she conceded, carefully. "Yes, I think we would both enjoy it."

"Good! So, as I said, we'll need to get Rose kitted out."

She took a deep breath. She was well and truly committed now. "There's an excellent sea and beach shop that's just opened at the end of the harbour. I bought some armbands for Rose in there and I've been taking her down to Pedi beach whenever I've had a couple of hours off duty during the day. She simply loves the water. As long as I'm by her side I know she's safe."

"So you'll take the armbands with you, won't you?"

"Of course!"

"How do you think Rose would be if we were to drop anchor in some quiet little bay on the Saturday night and she could sleep on the boat?"

Heavens! Once more she stared at him as she tried to sort out her confused feelings. On the one hand she found herself longing to say yes. The thought of a whole weekend! With her track record, did she dare?

"Give yourself time to think it over," he said amiably as he watched her, realising she was having deep reservations about this. Do you have a portable cot we could take with us for Rose? If not, we could buy one when we get her life jacket."

"Yes, I have a travel cot."

She looked up at him suddenly realising it had taken him a great deal of courage to ask her and Rose out for a whole weekend. They were after all just good friends. She shouldn't misinterpret the situation. It was a kindly, friendly gesture and he would be disappointed if she turned the idea down.

She told herself to stop taking the idea so seriously. Yannis wasn't the sort of man to take advantage of her. Not unless she made it clear she wanted him to—which she was determined not to do!

She smiled and began speaking quickly and enthusiastically before she could change her mind. "Yes, I think Rose would really enjoy a weekend on the boat. The cot doubles as a play pen if we want to let her play on deck without having to hold her all the time and…" She paused to draw breath. "And I think I'm going to enjoy it as well!"

He put out his arms and drew her against him. "And I think I love your enthusiasm for life. It's sort of…infectious."

She could feel herself revelling in the feeling of his muscular body against hers. So much for trying to stay cool! She really should pull herself away. There was nothing platonic about the way he was holding her.

She looked up at him, still feeling, oh, so comfortable in his embrace, not even daring to move in case she broke the magic spell that seemed to be binding them together. His eyes were shining with excitement. She'd never seen him so fired up.

He bent his head and kissed her, gently at first and then with more urgency as if he couldn't get enough of her. She could feel him moving his body closer to hers so that they fitted exactly together.

Someone was knocking on the door.

She tried to break away but he held her tighter for a moment before reluctantly loosening the circle of his arms.

"Dr Karavolis?"

"Yes. I'm coming!"

The door opened. As the newest doctor to have joined the hospital walked in, all he saw was a couple of senior doctors looking less than welcoming at his interruption.

"I'm sorry to interrupt you, sir," he said nervously. "You asked me to come and see you this morning. I didn't know…"

"That's OK, Stamatis. Dr Cathy is just leaving."

Dr Cathy was definitely leaving! Feeling hot and flustered, Cathy tried to stay calm until she was outside the door. It was a long time since she'd actually blushed! But it did make her feel very young again. Almost a teenager.

As she walked down the corridor she was thinking she would have to get her reactions to Yannis under control if she was to spend a whole weekend on the boat with him. And she would most certainly have to strengthen her resolve!

Yannis ran a hand through his hair as he sat down behind his desk, desperately trying to look as if he was in charge of the situation.

"Do sit down, Stamatis."

He motioned to the chair at the other side of the desk.

"I've brought the papers you asked for, Dr Karavolis."

"Please, call me Yannis. We're working together now as colleagues. I've been impressed with the work you've done in the four weeks you've been here. Especially yesterday evening when you took over that orthopaedic operation. I've seen the patient this morning and the post-operative X-rays show you made an excellent job of plating his tibia."

"Thank you...er...Yannis. I'm very interested in orthopaedic surgery and since I qualified I've spent a great deal of time working in orthopaedics."

Yannis glanced down at the personal papers Stamatis had brought him. He'd seen the duplicates when he'd first arrived but he liked to check the originals of all new staff and simply hadn't had the time during the past weeks.

"Yes, we were both trained at the same medical school in Athens," Yannis said, smiling as he looked up at the eager young doctor. "So what made you want to come to work at a hospital on Ceres when you were in line for a good career in Athens?"

"I had already applied to come here when we were alerted to the fact that you needed extra staff. Now that I've been taken on sooner than I'd hoped for, I would very much like to stay on here. You see, I have family connections here. My father died a few months ago and I feel it my duty to take care of my mother. I'm her only son."

"So were you born here?"

"Yes."

"So was I. I think coming back to your roots can be very healing when you've suffered a bereavement. It helps to put life in perspective. You've probably had to sacrifice some of your ambitious ideas but there's certainly a place for you here, Stamatis."

The young man swallowed hard. "You mean you'll give me a contract?"

"I'll certainly recommend you to the board of governors. Your contract should go through as a matter of course."

Yannis stood up and came round the desk, holding out his hand. "Welcome to the team, Stamatis."

"Thank you, Yannis. Thank you very much for all the help you've given me."

Yannis sat silently at his desk after the young doctor left him alone again. Only twenty-eight years old but full of promise. Just as he'd been ten years ago. No girlfriend apparently. He'd soon find someone here on the island. He didn't seem to have any hang-ups in that direction.

Whereas he was starting out on a romantic journey with so many memories from the past to contend with. How would he deal with romance and guilt at the same time? And how could he make sure he didn't hurt Cathy while he was getting himself sorted out?

She'd become very precious to him. Cathy—and little Rose. A mother and a daughter all on their own. And he was a man without a wife. It could be the most perfect combination if only he could find out how to let go of the past and move on.

CHAPTER SIX

BY the time they were leaving the jetty in front of Yannis's house Rose had become decidedly fractious. Having been taken down to the shop in the harbour during the morning and slotted into a variety of life jackets, none of which had proved to be ideal for such a small child, she was now in a non-cooperative mood.

"She's tired," Cathy said, as Rose's wailing continued, even though she was being rocked gently in her mother's arms.

"Rose will be fine when we get out on the water and we can let her loose in her play pen," Yannis said confidently, turning round from the wheel to view his two guests huddled at the back of the boat.

He was thinking that he was glad that he'd chosen to buy a motor boat instead of a larger vessel that would have been reliant on sails and the need for an experienced crew. This boat was very easy to manage so he'd be able to concentrate on keeping his inexperienced crew happy. Once they got out of the narrow part of the inlet.

A large ferry was coming across from Rhodes, making its way into Ceres harbour. He slowed so as not to get too near. Even so, he caught the full blast of the wash several seconds later as the waves rippled towards him. He turned into the waves and rode through them. It was a choppy ride!

"Whoops! Nothing I could do about that, Cathy. Is Rose OK?"

"She's nearly asleep. We had an early start today and then that long session in the shop was very tiring. I did take her in a couple of days ago and the man promised to get some smaller sizes in for me. But apparently they didn't have them in stock over in Rhodes."

"Don't worry, I've made sure she's secured into the one we bought. There should be a smaller one in the next delivery and we can get that one."

Cathy moved further into the cabin, cradling the now sleeping Rose in her arms. Yannis had one hand on the wheel and was turning round to talk to her. They were out on a wider stretch of water now, though still hugging the coastline. Rose, having made such a fuss at being made to wear the wretched jacket, had now fallen into a deep sleep, snuffling through her crocodile tears.

Cathy had been impressed with the way Yannis had taken charge of everything when they'd been in the shop. The shop assistant had been profusely apologetic that the expected supplies hadn't turned up. His boss had made a special urgent order. "No, sorry, sir, he's not here at the moment... Yes, I'll tell him you're not pleased about that, sir... Of course... If there's anything else I can help you with..."

They'd come out of the shop with the jacket and several toys that Yannis had insisted on buying for Rose. "To keep her happy in the play pen." He'd taken care of payment and had brushed aside Cathy's efforts to make a contribution. Yannis seemed to be the only person in the shop enjoying himself.

She'd been so looking forward to this weekend that she realised maybe she'd expected everything to run smoothly. Now that Rose was quiet again, she could begin to relax. And worry!

Worry that she'd brought the wrong clothes for both of them. Too many obviously. She always packed too much, especially when she was nervous of the occasion. But would it matter out here?

She moved to the stern of the boat so that she was just outside the cabin, still holding Rose tightly in her arms. Leaning back, she turned her face up towards the sun. Carefully she allowed one arm to dip over the side of the boat towards the spray that was coming up from the sea as they sped across the water.

Mmm, this was the life! But she'd glimpsed the tiny cabin as Yannis had been stowing their bags away. Hmm, not much room in there! There was a tiny alcove at the end of the cabin where Yannis had said he would erect Rose's cot and he'd explained that the two bunks at either side of the cabin opened out into a full-size double bed.

She'd felt he'd been testing her out when he'd said that. She knew he'd been watching her reaction but she hadn't made any comment or even dared to look at him. Yes, they were both nervous! She would deal with the situation later, keeping her head, not listening to her heart, remembering the past.

"Are you two OK out there, Cathy?"

"I'm fine! Rose is completely out for the count. And how about you?"

"Excellent! We'll be stopping for lunch soon."

The sea was now completely calm again. She watched as Yannis steered the boat into a small bay with steep hillsides falling down into the deep water. No one in sight. Bliss!

"I feel we're playing Robinson Crusoe," she said as Yannis cut the engine so that they could glide alongside the small stone jetty. "I remember coming here with my mother when I was younger. There's a small deserted chapel up on the side of the hill, as I recall. There was a sheep that had got locked inside it by mistake and Mum persuaded it to come outside and drink some water."

"Childhood memories are so precious. Here, let me take Rose while you get yourself ashore. Do you want to change on board for swimming first?"

She handed over the sleeping Rose and slipped into the cabin, searching out her bag and struggling into the new bikini she'd bought as soon as she'd agreed to this weekend. Black and white, couldn't go wrong with that. At least the marine shop had come up trumps in that respect.

By the time she got to the shore, Yannis was

sitting on the sand, talking quietly to her daughter who was staring up at him in half-awake fascination with this man she'd begun to like enormously.

"Yaya," she said, stroking her fingers through his hair.

"She's trying so hard to say Yannis," Cathy said, spreading a couple of towels on the beach as she joined them. "Yaya is her approximation."

"It's a difficult name to say for one so young. It's the Y sound at the beginning that gets her. Wow!" He was looking at her new bikini now, admiration gleaming in his eyes. "I like that! But I like the look of who's wearing it even better."

How long had it been since he'd paid a compliment to a woman? she wondered as she felt a glow of pleasure spreading over her.

"Are you going to swim in your new bikini or is it too precious?"

"Of course I'm going to swim in it." She stood up. "I'll put Rose's armbands on and she can come in with me."

"She's only just waking up. Why not let her come round slowly? We'll have a nice little chat while you swim. And I can admire you from here, looking like a sea nymph."

She laughed. "You've got a good imagination. OK, if you're happy holding Rose..."

It was an offer she couldn't refuse, she thought as she ran to the outcrop of rocks at the corner of the bay. She remembered it so well from the times she'd been here as a child. Her mother had taught her to dive here.

"It's quite safe from here, Cathy," she'd told her as she'd explained how to put her arms in the correct diving shape above her head. "Now, bend forward and I'll tip you in when you're ready... There we go!"

As she stood on the rock and looked down into the deep water she could hear her mother's voice again, urging her on and then gently tipping her over.

She dived now, down, down into the cold depths, so refreshing, so energising. She rose to the surface and lay on her back, looking up at the blue sky, with not a cloud in sight. Turning towards the shore, she could see two pairs of eyes glued on her.

Yannis waved. "Spectacular display! Are you training for the Olympics?"

"Of course! Come on in, the pair of you. It's

wonderful! Rose's armbands are in my bag there beside you."

Soon Yannis was swimming out on his back with the armbanded Rose on his chest. Cathy swam to meet them.

"Mama!"

Rose could hardly contain her excitement at meeting her mother in the sea like this.

They had a picnic lunch when they were all back on the shore. Cathy had been to the bakery on the corner of the Ceres harbour by the bridge and bought spanakopita, spinach pies and teropita, cheese pies. Yannis had bought far too many tomatoes at the fruit and veg shop.

"Just in case we get marooned out there for the summer," he'd told Cathy.

And, of course, Cathy had got too many freshly baked bread rolls simply because she loved the smell and had got carried away.

They were huddled together on two towels, eating as if they were starving. Rose had discovered the delights of a ripe misshapen Mediterranean tomato and was enjoying the feeling of the juice dribbling down from her mouth to her chin. She tried without success to bend her tongue down to catch some of the delicious dribble but it escaped down onto her bare chest.

Reaching down, she rubbed it over her skin and smiled as she admired the lovely red colour her chest now had.

She was now babbling happily.

Yannis went down to the sea and lifted the bottle of wine from the pool he was using as a wine cooler. Touching the bottle against the side of his face, he nodded.

"That's better. Anyone for a glass of wine?"

Cathy held out her empty glass. "Yes, please."

He sank down beside her, his sandy body close against hers. "I thought I would cook supper this evening when the sun's gone down."

"You're going to cook?"

"Well, of course I'm going to cook! I'm not just the captain of this ship, you know. I have to double as ship's cook."

"And what am I?"

A wicked grin was hovering on his lips as he leaned forward, kissing her gently on the side of the cheek.

"You, my dear, are the cabaret, brought on board for the captain's pleasure."

"Oh, sir! You'll have to tell me what your

pleasure is," Cathy teased him back, trying to keep the mood light.

"I haven't decided yet."

"Mama, mama!" Rose demanded more attention and insisted on putting herself between them.

"I know the role you can play tonight," Yannis whispered to Cathy over the top of Rose's head. "You can be chief nursemaid and rock the baby to sleep while the cook prepares the food for the captain's table. Then when the baby is sleeping the captain and the cabaret can have the rest of the evening to themselves."

"Sounds good to me. You're on!"

They spent the rest of the day in and out of the water. Rose was beside herself with happiness, having the full attention of her mother and this wonderful man who'd come into their lives, making it so much more interesting.

They all watched the sunset together, Cathy holding small sunglasses over Rose's eyes.

"Rose doesn't really need these," she whispered to Yannis. "Her eyes are already closed."

"I noticed that myself," Yannis said as he snuggled close to the pair of them, his arm surrounding their tight little huddle at the edge of the shore.

The sun was dipping low in the sky, making wide swathes of crimson and gold over the smooth surface of the sea. It seemed to pause for a short time as if contemplating its dive into the deep water, elongating its lower side until it resembled a golden aubergine, before taking the final plunge.

"It's gone!" Cathy breathed, as awestruck as she had always been when she'd witnessed the uncanny sunset ritual. "As a child I couldn't understand how the sun could go down in one place and come up the next morning in another. However many times my mother explained to me about the earth being round, I still preferred to imagine it sitting at the bottom of the sea, deciding where and when it would emerge and spread its fantastic light again."

He drew her towards him. "Oh, Cathy, don't ever change. I hope you'll always keep your charm. I've become immune to the simple happiness that occurs every day if you look for it. I'm still hoping it will come back again when…when I'm able to forget."

She turned her face upwards towards him and

saw the anguish that had reappeared in his eyes as unpleasant memories flooded back. Even after the wonderful day they'd enjoyed together the pain of bereavement was still just under the surface, waiting to erupt and spoil the moment for him.

A cool breeze blew across the shore. His arm tightened around them. He would so like to imagine that this was his family. This beautiful woman who'd come into his life and made such a difference already…and who knew what a great difference she would make in the future? And this gorgeous, magical child who'd arrived with no input from himself, but already he felt as if she was a part of him.

"Let's go on board," he said gently. "You go ahead and start putting Rose to bed. I've erected the cot in the alcove off our cabin. I'll gather up our things from the beach and bring them on board."

She was singing an age-old lullaby as he pulled up the steps that led from the boat down onto the jetty. It was an English song he remembered his mother teaching him when he was a child. The words had sounded foreign when he was small but he'd loved the tune. He hummed along to it now, very quietly because he was sure that Rose would already be asleep and Cathy was simply making sure.

"Rock-a-bye baby on the tree top…"

She smiled up at him as he stood in the doorway of the cabin, putting a finger to her lips so that he wouldn't speak.

He sank down on the bed he'd prepared using the two bunk beds, watching his new miracle family. Their eyes met and locked in a contented gaze, each thinking how they were experiencing one of the rare moments of pure magic that sometimes occurred in life.

Rose's breathing had settled at last into the slow, peaceful sleep of childhood.

"She's off," Cathy said quietly, standing up. He reached out and drew her down beside him.

For a few seconds they both remained still, simply looking into each other's eyes.

Cathy broke the precious silence. "You know, I was thinking just now how wonderful it is to be spending a Saturday evening in such an idyllic situation. Remembering all the times I used to make such an effort to be busy-busy, going out to noisy places, loud music, chattering people… and here we are, nothing but the murmur of the waves lapping against the side of the boat."

She sighed as she lay back in his arms. She knew she was giving in to temptation but her treacherous body was trying to overcome her resistance. Mmm, it had been a long time since…

"Everything depends on who you're with," he said quietly, nuzzling his lips against her hair. "That's nice! Don't wash your hair when you're in the shower. I love the smell of the sea water."

She laughed. "And the jam from Rose's sticky fingers as she ate her supper."

"And you, just you, that wonderful certain, indefinable aura that follows you everywhere."

"Ever thought of becoming a poet?"

He grinned. "Ah, but I couldn't be a poet unless I had a beautiful woman in my arms to write about."

"I don't know about beautiful. I feel in desperate need of a shower. Would you show me how to work that weird and wonderful shower in that tiny wet cubicle?"

"I'll give you a personal demonstration…soon… when you really need it…when…"

He was punctuating his words with kisses. Lingering on the final kiss as he savoured the taste of her salty lips and lost himself entirely in the sensual waves that were coursing through his body. He could feel her reciprocating, moving her wonderful, sexy, delicious body into the momentum that had started up between them.

He knew beyond a shadow of a doubt that there was no going back now. He could no longer contain his desperate longing for her, no longer think about the consequences of his love-making. His heart was telling him that this was, oh, so right for both of them…

She lay back against the rumpled sheets and looked up at the wooden roof of the cabin. Her body felt totally different somehow. Sort of liquid, languid, completely boneless. Just a mass of sensual nerves, heightened and tuned to perfection. Their love-making had been so heavenly, so completely abandoned, totally spur of the moment yet indefinably out of this world.

She sighed with contentment. "I feel utterly ravished!"

He laughed. "Is that good or bad?"

"Mmm, good, I think." She turned on her side to look at him. "What about you?"

"On a scale of one to ten?"

"Yes."

"Eleven."

She grinned. "Me too."

As he held her close in his arms she realised that she was keeping up her light-hearted banter to make sure he didn't start thinking serious thoughts about whether it was right or not. This was a milestone in their relationship. Making love together in a light-hearted way, each giving themselves and holding nothing back. But she didn't want him to read anything too deep into it. Didn't want him to feel the slightest bit guilty.

"About that shower," she said, moving out the circle of his arms. "I definitely need one now."

"Me too!" He put out his hand to help her off the bed and into the tiny cubicle. "It's going to be a squeeze but you'll never be able to cope without my help."

"Oh, I think I could manage by myself." She was now flattened against the side of the shower, unable to move because Yannis's chest was hard against her.

"Spoilsport! Of course you couldn't shower by yourself." He turned on the tap and water was pumped up from the tank with a loud gurgling sound. "Stop wriggling so I can soap your back and make you think I'm totally indispensable in this operation."

She began giggling uncontrollably. "Don't! You're tickling me, you're…"

He silenced her with a long hard kiss as the water coursed over them both and their bodies became totally entwined again…

Afterwards, enveloped in large fluffy towels, they lay back on the bed, fingers locked together, breathing rhythmically as they both closed their eyes, thinking their separate thoughts about what had just happened.

Cathy was the first to speak. She was anxious to keep up the momentum of their light-hearted togetherness.

"I'm feeling ravenously hungry. Are you still going to cook me supper, Captain?"

"Of course. So long as you'll provide the cabaret."

"That was the cabaret."

"In that case, I'd like some more." He was already gathering her up into his arms again.

"Later," she told him in a playful tone.

He flung a dry towel round his waist and stepped out into the galley. "Don't want to burn my vital organs while I'm cooking."

"Absolutely not!"

She dug deep into the bag she'd brought with her and found a flimsy sarong. Winding it round her body, she secured it so it wouldn't fall down—unless someone pulled it away, which was a definite possibility!

There was no mirror in the cabin. Pointless to try and see in her small hand make-up mirror. She'd no idea how she looked but decided that Yannis seemed to like the natural look. Damp hair, no make-up, salty lips. He'd told her he found that very sexy. Maybe she should have another dip in the sea. But that would mean another shower and who knew where that would lead to?

He turned from the stove as she walked barefoot from the cabin to the galley, three steps in total.

"Hope I'm not late."

"Perfect timing. You look stunning!" He leaned across and kissed the side of her cheek. "I hope you like Chinese food."

She perched on the stool beside the stove. "Chinese food cooked by a Greek doctor while we're marooned in a deserted moonlit bay. Absolutely perfect! Where did you learn to cook Chinese food?"

He tossed some narrow strips of beef into the

pan and began stir-frying them with the vegetables already in there.

"Would you pass me that soy sauce by the sink
there…? Thanks. My father taught me. He was a
sailor before I was born and from the stories he
told me he'd been everywhere in the world many
times over. He was much older than my mother
and family life came to him after many years of
travels. So he was a fantastic storyteller and a
fantastic cook."

"You told me your mother was a widow
when she died. How old were you when your
father…?"

"I was twelve. My mother and I were heartbroken but I had to be the strong one. The man of
the house from then on. When I got my place at
medical school in Athens she closed up the house
and came with me, living in a rented flat. After a
couple of years she said she was missing Ceres.
She didn't like the hustle and bustle of Athens.
So I helped her to return and open up the house
again. I arranged for her to have a housekeeper
to take care of her and I came over to see her as
often as I could."

He put down his spatula on the wooden chopping board. "It's ready now. If you sit across the table I'll keep this place nearer the stove."

He poured some wine into their glasses. "Are you OK with chopsticks?"

"Of course! I love Chinese food and it always tastes better with chopsticks. This is absolutely delicious! If you get bored with being a doctor you could always open a restaurant."

He gave her a sexy grin. "Only if you'll do the cabaret."

"Ah, but that's by special arrangement."

She looked across the table at this gorgeous hunk of manhood and felt a sensual stirring deep down inside. His hairy chest, the towel loosely slung around his waist made him look so very desirable.

She just knew there was going to be the most fantastic climax at the end of this evening. It was inevitable. The two of them together in that tiny cabin. Couldn't she allow herself to have just one night of fantasy?

She'd checked on Rose before she'd come into the galley. Her daughter was blissfully asleep and likely to stay that way after the tiring day she'd experienced. So it would be just the two of them all night long.

Suddenly she felt nervous. She took a deep breath as she told herself to keep it light, go with the flow. Yes, she was playing with fire but it was all part of the fantasy.

"Yannis, you've got a bean sprout sticking to your chest."

He laughed as he glanced down and deftly picked it up with his chopsticks. "Good thing I hadn't changed into my dress shirt."

"It would have looked out of place with that towel you're wearing. I love the colour of it."

"Sort of greyish white. Yes, I chose it most carefully."

He sighed contentedly. This was an evening he was going to remember for a long time. It was good to find he was enjoying life to the full again. What a difference Cathy was making to his life. And little Rose, taking the place of…no, not taking the place of his little son but definitely helping the healing process.

He poured more wine, leaning back against the cooker to get a better view of the beautiful woman across the table. This had been the most relaxed meal he'd eaten since he'd been with Maroula. In some ways Cathy was like Maroula, in other ways she was completely different. But in the most important way she filled that awful void that had been with him since Maroula's death.

The candle on the table was flickering. He knew he ought to get up and change it before it went out but he didn't want to break the peaceful ambience that existed between them. The way she was sitting, completely quiet and relaxed, content just to be with him.

She was exactly like Maroula had been on the night when she'd told him he was going to be a father. They'd been sitting in their little kitchen and he'd cooked a stir-fry because she loved Chinese food.

He leaned forward now, reaching towards the beautiful slim hand on the table. "Mar…" He stopped himself, realising he'd just made an unforgivable mistake.

He'd been speaking his wife's name softly. For one brief moment in time he'd thought that Cathy was Maroula. Maybe she hadn't heard him? He swallowed hard as he gazed at her. Had she heard?

Cathy's eyes flickered as she allowed her hand to stay in his grasp. Should she comment on his slip of the tongue? Was that all it was, a slip of the tongue? Or was Yannis wishing that she was

Maroula, that he could turn the clock back? When they made love had he been pretending that…?

She stood up quickly, unable to pursue that awful line of thought. "I'll just check on Rose," she said quietly.

He watched her bending her head to go down into the cabin, heard the swish of her sarong as she passed along the side of the bed where they'd made love. Had he blown it with Cathy?

He stood up and snuffed out the end of the candle, reaching up to the locker above the sink to find a fresh one. He would have it burning brightly by the time Cathy returned.

She seemed to be taking a long time.

Cathy leaned over the side of Rose's cot and tucked the sheet over the baby's plump arm.

"Night-night, my precious," she whispered. "I'll always have you, whatever happens to me."

She gripped the side of the cot.

It was all just too close to home for her. She'd been here before. Dave had called out his wife's name in the night on two occasions. As he'd lain dreaming beside her, she'd distinctly hear him say "Maggie". And she remembered how devastated, how jealous she'd been, even though at that time the lying, cheating Dave had told her his wife had left him.

When Yannis had begun to say Maroula's name she'd had exactly the same reaction. That meant her feelings for Yannis were becoming too strong. She'd vowed not to lose her heart to any man ever again after the way she'd been treated in the past. She was too trusting! Yannis probably just saw her as a diversion to his ordinary life. Ultimately that's all she'd been to Dave.

She should have learned by now that all men would disappoint her in time. Even her own father. So she'd got to be careful not to let Rose get too attached to Yannis. Men came into your lives and left when it suited them. Once again she vowed that she wouldn't put Rose through what she'd been through in her childhood.

No, it was time to rethink their situation and go back to their platonic relationship. Business as usual when they were in hospital working together.

She walked back through the cabin and saw him sitting dejectedly, staring at the new candle.

His face lit up as she stood in the doorway. "Is Rose OK?"

"She's fine. I think she'll sleep all night. She was completely whacked out when I put her down."

"It's all that fresh sea air."

"Yes, I feel tired myself now, so I think I'll turn in, just in case I do have to get up in the night to see to Rose. Goodnight, Yannis."

"Goodnight, Cathy."

He half rose to reach out for her, but she had hurried back into the cabin.

He sank back on his chair and stared into the candlelight.

CHAPTER SEVEN

As she sat waiting for the next patient to arrive, Cathy had a few moments to reflect on the situation between herself and Yannis. Three weeks had passed since they'd spent that weekend on the boat together.

It had been idyllic until the whole atmosphere had changed at suppertime in the tiny galley. She'd finally come to her senses and stopped the role play that had allowed her to be so provocative. She knew she'd gone over the line she'd drawn for herself and was in danger of history repeating itself. When she'd heard Yannis beginning to say his wife's name she'd known she'd been a fool—again!

She remembered how she'd lain awake, feigning sleep when Yannis had finally come to bed. Before he'd arrived she'd heard him going out on the deck, probably staying there until he felt it was safe to come into the cabin.

And when Rose had woken up crying in the

middle of the night she'd known that Yannis had almost been relieved that they could focus all their attention on the distraught child. Cathy had checked her daughter's temperature. They'd both agreed it was slightly raised and that they would head back to Ceres harbour in the morning.

Cathy had suspected that the heat of the cabin and the unfamililiarity of the surroundings were causing this slight discomfort to her daughter. And she'd guessed that Yannis had also come to the same conclusion and had been glad of the excuse to get back to the normality of his bachelor freedom.

"*Kali mera*, Cathy."

She smiled as her next patient was wheeled into her small office.

"*Kali mera*, Ariadne. So, how've you been since I last saw you?"

She took Ariadne's notes from the nurse who'd wheeled her in. She knew already from her perusal of the state of Ariadne's health on the computer that there was a further problem with this mother of three. She had symphysis pubis caused by the loosening of the ligaments which held the pubic bones in their correct position.

"I've had a lot of pain, Cathy."

Cathy watched her patient as she clutched the sides of her wheelchair. She didn't look at all well. She glanced at the results of the ultrasound scan she'd had that morning, which had taken longer than expected and was the reason she'd had some time to herself just now.

Cathy took a deep breath as she read the scribbled notes Yannis had put at the bottom of the page. Apparently, he'd been called to look at Ariadne's scan and was on his way to discuss the best course of action.

"Under the circumstances it would be unwise to allow the pregnancy to continue," he'd written.

What did he mean? Was he contemplating....?

"Yannis!" She looked up from the notes as he arrived.

"I was in Theatre when I got called down here to Ariadne's ultrasound. I've got to go back but I thought we should discuss this."

He smiled at their patient. "How's the pain now, Ariadne? Any better since I gave you the painkiller?"

Ariadne shook her head. "I don't know how much more I can take, Yannis. Some days I can't move without my whole body going into spasm.

Are my twins OK in there? They're not being harmed, are they?"

"No, they're perfectly safe inside your womb, Ariadne. But all things considered, I think it best we get them out as soon as possible."

The patient's eyes widened. "You mean...?"

"You're thirty-six weeks pregnant, almost full term. The twins are definitely viable if we deliver them today."

"Today?" Ariadne's face registered her relief that the end of the ordeal was in sight.

"In fact, this morning." Yannis looked across at Cathy. "I've arranged for Stamatis, who was assisting me in Theatre, to finish off the suturing. I'll get someone to finish your list here so that you can come with me to the obstetrics department and assist me there. Is that OK with you?"

"Of course."

They'd discussed Ariadne's case several times during the last few weeks and both had already agreed that if there were any complications they would operate immediately. And Yannis had remembered that Cathy had particularly requested she be involved in the birth if possible.

Ariadne raised a feeble hand in the air and

touched Yannis's arm. "Will it be painful, Yannis?"

"I'll give you a Caesarean section under general anaesthetic. It will be much less painful than trying to get you in position to administer an epidural, the surgery will be really quick and I promise you won't feel a thing."

"Will you get somebody to call my husband? He's had to go off to Rhodes today on business. He's told me all the way through this pregnancy he would try to be at the birth if I went into labour early. But, to be honest, I think he'll be relieved to miss this. He's been with me for the first three and found them pretty harrowing. He fainted for our first, had to leave the room for the next two, so…"

Cathy smiled. "So we'll just get on without him, shall we? I'll give him a call now to let him know what's going on."

They stood either side of the operating table in the obstetrics department. With a gloved hand, she handed Yannis a scalpel and watched as he made an incision across Ariadne's abdomen. As he skilfully cut through the abdominal muscles she was almost holding her breath. It was strange how some patients came to mean such a lot to you. She'd bonded with this plucky mother of three, soon to be mother of five—hopefully.

Yannis's hands were now inside the womb, carefully lifting out the first blood-covered baby. Cathy leaned over to take it from him as Theatre Sister stepped forward to take delivery of the second.

Cathy's baby was the first to utter the desired squawk that signified life. The cord was cut. She handed the baby to the midwife standing beside her.

"A boy and a girl this time," Yannis said, smiling across at Cathy. "Ariadne didn't want to know what they were. She said as long as they were fit and healthy she didn't care. She's already got a boy and two girls so she'll be happy with these little ones."

"Not so little either," Cathy said. "Both a good size for thirty-six weeks. Ariadne will be glad to be relieved of the weight. This should ease the strain on the ligaments and help the pubic bones to get back to their correct position."

Cathy looked down at Ariadne who was still anaesthetised, completely unaware that the operation had been a success. Lucky woman, five children and a loving husband!

Yannis looked across at Cathy. "It's time you were going off duty, Cathy. I scheduled you for a free afternoon. I'm almost finished here and the theatre staff will assist me."

"Thanks. I'm looking forward to spending it with Rose."

"That's what I thought." He bent his head and continued suturing.

She went into the anteroom and peeled off her gloves, staring into the mirror above the sink as she washed her hands. The face in the mirror looked strained. Yes, she definitely needed to spend more time with Rose.

She flung her gown into the bin and set off across the room towards the corridor door. The door from Theatre opened and Yannis came through. She turned in surprise.

"Finished already?"

He gave her a wry grin. "Yes. When I dismissed you just now I didn't say I'd given myself the same afternoon off duty."

Her heartbeat accelerated. "Why?" Oh what a stupid thing to say! "I mean, won't you be required to…?"

"Everything's under control here. The postnatal team is taking over. We'll be back early this evening to check on Ariadne and her new twins when she's fully awake again. Well, at least I will. I haven't checked on what your plans for the afternoon are. I scheduled you to take the outpatient clinic that starts at six so you may wish to come back later than me."

"Well, I was simply going to play with Rose and give her some quality time."

"Could I share in the quality time with you? I've hardly seen the pair of you since that unfortunate flick of temperature Rose had on the boat meant we had to come back early. Would you like to come out to the house? Eleni will rustle up some lunch for the three of us."

Cathy swallowed hard and reviewed the situation. Having ignored her for three weeks, why was he suddenly inviting her for lunch? This was exactly how Dave had been, except he would disappear completely for a few weeks and then reappear with flowers and chocolates, trying to woo her back again. Well, she wasn't going to be wooed back by the offer of lunch. She'd renewed her vow to stick with their platonic relationship, hadn't she?

As he watched her he could see there was some kind of conflict going on. "Cathy, it's only lunch I'm suggesting. And I'd love to see Rose again. I haven't seen her for ages and we had such a marvellous time swimming in the sea together. What's the problem?"

If he only knew! Did she dare allow Rose to start bonding again with Yannis? A small voice inside her head was now saying it would do her daughter such a lot of good to spend the afternoon with both of them. After all, she was only speculating that Yannis was the same as all the other men who'd passed through her life, wasn't she? She could be wrong about him, couldn't she?

She took a deep breath. "Yes, that would be most enjoyable, Yannis," she said politely.

He smiled with relief. "Good! I've got the car in the car park so we'll go up to Chorio and pick up Rose."

Eleni was delighted to see her again, asking her where she'd been, fussing over Rose, carrying her on one hip while she finished setting the table in the garden room overlooking the shore.

"No, you sit still, Cathy," Eleni insisted as she gave Rose another biscuit to suck and scatter crumbs around. "You've been working in hospital all morning and I've enjoyed my morning out here.

"I've cooked your favourite vegetable soup, Yannis, as you asked me to. Enough for the two of you. I remember you told me this morning. But I've made enough for Rose just in case she came along as well. I'll put it through the blender and cool it for her. Maybe it would be better if I fed her in the kitchen. It's too hot out here."

"I find it nice and shady under the trees," Cathy said. "And there's a nice breeze from the water."

Yannis was giving her a meaningful look, indicating she leave the decision to Eleni. As soon as they were alone he explained that Eleni liked nothing better than to have sole charge of a baby.

"Eleni rarely gets her chance to have a small baby to herself. Even her grandchildren are growing up too quickly for her. She'll spoil Rose rotten but that's no bad thing. I don't think you can give too much love to children. As long as they feel secure, that's one of the most important things in life."

She leaned against the cushions in the high-backed wicker chair and looked out across the water to the steep hill at the other side of the inlet. It had only been a few weeks since she'd spent the night here but it seemed like a lifetime ago. She had to admit she'd hoped she would be invited back here. But she'd had no idea how complicated it was going to be.

"This is such a lovely garden room," she said, looking around her at the low fence separating this area from the rest of the garden. "You've even got a fridge for the drinks over there."

She took a sip of her fresh lime soda.

"I don't use it often enough. It's a lunchtime sort of place. More ice in your drink?"

He returned from the fridge with a bowl of ice cubes just as Eleni came out from the kitchen carrying a tureen of soup. She set it down on the table together with some home-baked bread rolls.

"Don't worry about Rose. Petros is taking care of her."

"Thank you, Eleni."

Yannis dipped the soup ladle into the tureen and gave Cathy a generous portion.

"That's far too much!"

"You haven't tasted it yet."

"Mmm! You're right. It's delicious. I can taste

courgettes, peppers, carrots, beans and wonderful herbs."

"All from the garden." He looked across the table. He'd been so nervous of setting up this lunch meeting but so far so good.

The ironic thing was that after that weekend together he'd realised that his affections were now totally centred on Cathy. That awful moment when he'd started to call her Maroula had given him just the momentum he'd needed to realise exactly what was now important to him. But Cathy's whole attitude towards him had changed after that.

He hadn't known how to treat her when they'd met in hospital. He'd been polite and professional but he hadn't dared to show any kind of warmth towards her. She'd seemed so cool and withdrawn. He'd even felt nervous of asking her to assist him this morning.

Cathy put down her spoon on the empty soup plate and looked across the table. Yannis was staring at her in such a serious way she was sure he was going to tell her some bad news.

"Is something wrong, Yannis?"

"Wrong? No, quite the reverse. I was just thinking…how…how wonderful it is to have you and Rose here today. I've missed you...both of you."

He reached across the table and took hold of her hand. "Cathy. Thank you for being so understanding. You've helped me so much to come to terms with my bereavement. I never thought I could move on and have a happy life again...until you came along and changed all that."

Eleni was coming across the lawn with a large wooden bowl of fruit, which she placed on their table.

"Rose is asleep on the kitchen sofa. Petros is sitting beside her so she'll come to no harm. I'll bring her out here when she wakes up."

Cathy smiled. "Thank you, Eleni. I'll come in soon and rouse her gently so that we have time to play on the shore under those trees. Our time together is so precious."

"You're so understanding, Cathy," Yannis said quietly, as soon as they were alone again. "You seem to realise what I'm going through in this transition from grieving widower to...well, how would you describe me now?"

She took a deep breath. "New man?"

He smiled, his eyes crinkling as he gazed at her. "That's what I'm aspiring to be...with your help. I've still got to get rid of the guilt I feel that I'm here getting on with my life and Maroula is no longer alive. Her life was cut short when she was in her prime and I'm happy again."

"Why should you feel guilty about that?"

"Sometimes I feel I could have prevented her death," he said quietly.

"The chances of that are remote," she replied evenly. "Even if you'd been driving the car, and the timing had been exactly the same, you couldn't have prevented a large lorry on a blind bend on the wrong side of the road smashing into you."

He closed his eyes and she could see the tears squeezing out from under his eyelids. He'd told her when she'd first met him that crying was something men didn't do. But she was convinced that it could be therapeutic. She put her arms tightly around him and held him close until his shaking body was still again. All the time she was trying to convince herself that she was just being a good friend but the feel of his strong body in such close contact was having a devastating effect on her confused emotions.

She put her head against his shoulder and lifted her eyes to his.

He looked down at her. "Cathy, how long do

you think it will take me to forget entirely and to get rid of the guilt?"

"I don't think you'll ever entirely forget," she said softly. "You don't need to forget. Just try not to dwell on the unpleasant aspects and the guilt."

"Easier said than done." He gave her a wry smile. "But I'll try. Because I would hate to think that this could spoil our relationship."

She remained quiet. It was obvious to her that Yannis's idea of their relationship was different from what she was trying to maintain. If she hadn't been hurt so many times before, this was the point at which she would begin to relax and enjoy thoughts of a future together. But she simply daren't think any further than one day at a time.

She stood up. "I'll go and wake Rose up."

"Cathy." He was on his feet beside her, drawing her against him. "Thank you so much for being here with me, for all the help and comfort you're giving me. You're right. I am a new man!"

He bent his head and kissed her gently on the lips. His kiss deepened. She drank in the sensual waves of passion that spread down from her lips throughout her whole body. Oh, yes, he was a new man all right. There was so much sexy, vibrant vitality in Yannis, not to mention that his hands were now beginning to drive her senses wild with anticipation.

She broke away, telling herself she mustn't give in to temptation. But looking up at him now, she recognised that she wanted him as much as he wanted her.

"Tonight?" he whispered, trying to gain control of himself again. "Could I bring you home after we both come off duty? I presume Rose will be staying at Anna's if you're working this evening."

"Well, yes, it's already arranged, but, Yannis…"

"Yes?"

She was struggling to get a grip on her emotions. But the sensual waves coursing through her body were driving her mad with desire. She remembered the way it had been on the boat when they'd made love before supper. They had been light-hearted, simply role playing, hadn't they? Couldn't she suspend her fears just for one night and enjoy being with Yannis? Have a whole night in which there was no past, no future, simply the present moment?

"Well then… Do we have a date for tonight?"

He took hold of her hand and led her across the lawn towards the kitchen door.

"I think we do," she said, feeling too weak to struggle against that tempting voice inside her head.

Rose squealed with delight when Cathy put her down on the sand and allowed her to crawl down towards the sea. She was wearing her armbands and knew very well that this meant swimming and splashing around in the big water.

"It's very deep further out," Yannis said, as he cradled Rose in his arms and trod water. I don't want her to do her doggy paddle out here. "I know she could drown in shallow water but it still seems more dangerous the further out we go. I wouldn't want anything to happen to our precious little one."

Cathy made no comment about Yannis calling her daughter "our precious little one".

She doubted if it had even registered on his mind. All his paternal instinct seemed to be focused on her daughter and that was therapeutic for him. She found herself praying that he wasn't going to disappear from their lives. That he would always be somewhere in the background so that

Rose would never get hurt. She'd allowed the bonding of Yannis and Rose to go too far now.

She did a swift turn-around. The dark depths of the water held a fascination for her but they were always dangerous and she knew from studying records that this stretch of water had claimed the lives of tourists who'd thought they'd had the strength to swim to the other side.

"Let's go back," she said. "Will you take Rose or shall I?"

"I'll take her."

He turned on his back and swam towards the shore, his muscular legs kicking strongly against the water. She swam breaststroke alongside but found it hard to keep up with him.

Rose, firmly held by Yannis on his chest, laughed with sheer happiness at the wild adventure she was having. Once again she'd got her mummy and this magical man who made their lives so much more exciting when he turned up occasionally. Not as often as she would like but it was always fun when it happened.

Dried off and de-sanded they had tea in the garden room. Petros brought out the new high chair which had miraculously appeared in the kitchen.

"When did that arrive?" Cathy asked as she strapped her wriggling daughter in.

Yannis pretended to look puzzled. "Oh, we've had it for ages, haven't we, Petros? It belonged—"

"No, Yannis. You asked me to collect it from that shop in Rhodes."

Petros, bewildered, set off back to the kitchen to tell his wife that Yannis was losing his memory.

When the ritual of jam sandwiches and cakes had been performed and Rose had been persuaded to eat something whilst enjoying the fun of crumbling and spreading jam with her fingers, Cathy gave her daughter a banana.

Concentrating hard, Rose, with a very serious expression on her face, unzipped the banana and peeled it halfway down before biting the top off.

"Very good!" Yannis said, with parental-style pride. "What a clever girl!"

Cathy smiled. "Well, I figure if baby monkeys can do it, my daughter should have the intelligence to work it out."

"Yes, but it needs hand-eye co-ordination."

"True. But Rose will be one in two weeks' time so…"

"Oh, Cathy, we must have a party!" Yannis said happily. "Would you like to have it here?"

Decisions! Decisions! Events were moving too quickly for her to keep up. "To be honest, I hadn't thought about a party. I don't know if my boss will give me time off. It's in the middle of the week and I'll have to ask him."

"Ask away and take a whole day off…take two…so will I."

"Hey, steady on, Yannis. Don't go to extremes."

Yannis took hold of her hand.

"Why not? A birthday is something to celebrate—especially the first one. Clever little Rose successfully survived nine months in her mummy's uterus and then navigated herself down the birth canal. And she's learned so much in twelve months, how to sit up, how to crawl… Very soon she'll be walking. Did you see how she was trying to pull herself up from the floor by holding onto that chair?"

Cathy's smile broadened. "Yannis, I do like you when you're in this…mood."

She'd been going to say paternal mood but had decided not to. If Rose was the substitution for the child he'd lost then that was something to be happy about. Anything that helped in the healing process was heaven sent.

Yannis glanced at his watch. "We'll have to go. I'll drive the car again so we can take Rose up to Anna's."

Cathy took a clean cloth from the outdoor sink and wiped the jam and banana bits from around Rose's mouth. Yannis was already thinking ahead to the hospital schedule for the evening. He was trying not to think any further to the time when he would bring Cathy back home with him.

Cathy too, was trying to concentrate on other things, thinking ahead to the clinic she was going to take and trying not to allow herself to think about the night ahead.

"Ready, Cathy?"

Yannis deftly undid the straps on the high chair and took charge of Rose. "We need to go right now if we're going to give ourselves time to spend with Ariadne and her newborn twins."

They reached hospital with a few minutes to spare, having delivered a tired but happy Rose to Anna, who welcomed her as always with a big hug.

Ariadne was propped up in bed, a twin cuddled

up on each side of her. The proud father was sitting in a chair, gazing fondly at the latest editions to his family.

"Isn't my wife just the most amazing woman, Yannis? And I understand you were there at the birth as well, Cathy. Pity I couldn't make it. Important business meeting, you know. Well, somebody has to pay the bills when there are all these mouths to feed."

Ariadne smiled indulgently at her husband.

Cathy and Yannis conferred with the midwife in charge before staying a short time to chat with Ariadne and her husband. Yes, Yannis assured them, they would love to go to the twins' christening party when they received an invitation in due course.

"So where will you be this evening, Yannis?" Cathy asked as they walked together down the corridor outside Obstetrics.

"In my office to begin with, hopefully. I've got a load of paperwork to catch up with and have even got my secretary to stay late to help me. So if you need me, you've only got to give me a call."

Cathy gave him a wry smile. "I'll be too busy to call you. My midweek outpatients clinic is developing into a social club. There are more patients than I can handle usually."

"I'll get you some help," he said, taking out his mobile.

She listened as he spoke briefly.

"There's a trained nurse on her way. She lives around in Vasilios bay and her husband is going to bring her into Ceres town in his boat. She's just waiting for the port authorities to clear them. There's been a strong wind but she assures me she'll be with you in half an hour. Can you manage till then?"

"Of course."

"I'll come and collect you about eight, then."

The outpatient clinic started at six and finished at eight. Patients made appointments at a time that suited them. At least, that was what was supposed to happen. But this being Ceres, the patients wandered in when they felt like it, knowing that the kind lady doctor wasn't the type who would turn them away if they didn't have an appointment and she never watched the clock.

The female population of the island who worked during the day or couldn't get away from the house without the children had learned over the couple of months that Cathy had been doing the evening clinic and that she was a very good doctor. And what was more, she was a female who understood female medical problems and was easy to talk to.

So this midweek outpatient clinic had become very popular with both young girls and older women and had turned into something of a social club. When she arrived just a few minutes before six there were already six women sitting in her waiting room.

"*Kali spera*, Cathy!"

"*Kali spera.*" She smiled as she went into her consulting room and turned on the computer. According to the information that appeared on the screen she had only three patients booked this evening and they weren't supposed to be here until after seven. Oh, well, she made a point of putting down names and medical case information after she'd treated a patient so all she had to do was make sure she knew who she was dealing with.

As long as the medical secretaries in the records department had kept up to date with putting the written case histories onto the computer she would be fine. But as she'd come to realise, some of her patients just enjoyed an evening out of the house and a good gossip with women of their own age.

She'd left her door wide open so that her patients could see she was soon going to be available for them to come in and pour out their troubles to her.

She went to the doorway and looked around the assembled ladies. "Who's coming in first this evening?"

"Daniella." By general consensus everyone had agreed that Daniella should be the first.

"So what can I do for you?" Cathy asked, when her young patient was seated in front of her. She'd closed her door now so as to give them some privacy. Her patients might discuss their most intimate problems with each other out there in the waiting room but here in the sanctity of the doctor's consulting room they liked everything to remain private.

"I've missed a period."

Cathy had already noticed the ungainly gait of her patient as she'd waddled in through the door. The loose clothing intended to camouflage her belly was doing nothing to hide the obvious advanced pregnancy.

"Just one, Daniella?"

"Well, probably a few more. I can't remember... Oh, Doctor, my mother's going to kill me when she..."

The tears ran down her cheeks as Daniella tried to stifle her sobs.

Cathy reached for the box of tissues with one hand and with the other she put her arm round her patient's shoulders.

She waited until the sobs subsided. Daniella wiped a tissue over her face and blew her nose vigorously.

"Have you tried to tell your mother?"

"No, I daren't. I think she might have guessed but she hasn't said anything. I live with my dad and his new wife on Rhodes but he's turned me out now he knows I'm going to have a baby.

"He just told me to go back to my mum. But I don't get on with my mum. I just arrived on the ferry this afternoon. I'll have to go to my mum's tonight because I've nowhere else to go. And she'll kill me!"

"I don't think she'll do that, Daniella. She'll be concerned about you but most mums get used to the idea that their daughter is going to have a baby."

"Not mine!"

"Have you seen a doctor on Rhodes?"

"No!"

"Does the father know you're having his baby?"

"I don't know who the father is. It was just one night out in Rhodes. I met him that evening. He was a tourist just staying there for a few nights. I went back to his hotel with him and it just happened."

Cathy took a deep breath. "How old are you, Daniella?"

"Sixteen."

Oh, no. It was getting worse. "How old were you when you spent the night with this man?"

"I was just sixteen. It was my birthday."

Thank goodness for that! Cathy was glad she wouldn't have to make a report to the police. Even so, this was definitely a case for Social Services. But first she must establish how far advanced this pregnancy was.

"I'd like you to lie down on the couch here so I can examine you, Daniella."

As Cathy helped her patient onto the examination couch her apprehension was growing by the second. The young girl was in obvious pain.

She groaned as she lifted her legs up and then shrieked as she floundered onto the surface of the couch.

"No, oh, no. Doctor it's been getting worse all day. On the boat the pain was awful. It's in my back now and down my legs. It's everywhere. What's happening to me?"

Cathy had a pretty good idea even before she pulled aside the voluminous camouflage and saw the swollen abdomen. She placed her hands on Daniella and checked the muscular spasms that were causing her so much pain. The poor child was already in labour. No time to scrub up or perform any of the usual preliminaries. This baby was hell-bent on getting out under its own steam.

She pulled Daniella's legs into a lithotomy position so that she could examine the birth canal. Oh, no! The baby's head was crowning already. She needed another pair of hands. Where was that nurse when she needed her?

"Don't push, Daniella. Just pant for the moment." Realising that here was a young girl with no ante-natal preparation, she began to show her how to pant. "Like this so that you don't start pushing, bearing down. You have to…"

Too late. The head was out now, Daniella simply giving in to her deep primaeval urge to push. Cathy's eyes widened in concern as she saw the umbilical cord wrapped around the baby's neck. She really needed another pair of hands now because Daniella was refusing to keep still, moving from side to side, trying to get the baby out of her body.

The panic button was across the other side of the room, as was the phone. Holding the cord away from the baby's neck with one hand, she got her mobile from her pocket with the other and punched in Yannis's name on her address book. At least she hoped it was Yannis's number but it was difficult for her to see at this angle.

"Dr Yannis here. How—?"

"Yannis, please come…" She dropped the phone on the couch as she deftly unwrapped the cord, using both hands this time.

She breathed a sigh of relief. "It's OK, you can push now, Daniella."

The door opened and Yannis came in. "What was it that—? Ah!" He looked down at the young girl, her whole body drenched in sweat.

Cathy was carefully wrapping the new baby in a dressing towel, handing her to the new mum.

"There you go, Daniella, you've got a little boy."

"Oh, thank you, Doctor! Oh, he's lovely. Look at his little eyes."

Daniella's groans had turned to shrieks of delight now.

Yannis was already on the phone to Obstetrics. "Yes, the baby has already arrived, Sister, so if you could just send someone down to take the patient and the newborn up to your department for postnatal checks, that would be excellent. She'll be staying in at least overnight. Dr Cathy will give you the case history as soon as she's prepared it."

"That was an unusual start to the evening," Cathy said, as she sank down on her consulting chair, having despatched the happy young mother and child to Obstetrics.

"I'll get the notes written up on the computer as soon as the nurse arrives."

"I've just had a phone call from her. There's a big storm in the north of the island and the port authorities have cancelled all boat movements."

"So she won't be coming?"

"Evidently not. I might be able to pull in a

nurse from another department if I rang round or I could help you myself."

"You?"

"Don't look so shocked. I am a qualified doctor, you know."

She smiled. "Well, that's what I mean. You're vastly over-qualified for the things I'm going to delegate to be done this evening."

"Try me. I've given my secretary a load of letters to write. All I've got to do is go back later and sign them and that's the paperwork finished for the day. I could do a further round of the patients but I've already delegated that to young Dr Stamatis, who's always pleased to fill in for me. So, the more I can help you here the quicker we'll get away this evening. We do have a date, if you remember."

She looked up at him. He was so close. "How could I forget?"

He kissed her gently on the lips. Pulling himself reluctantly away, he looked down into the shining blue eyes that were gazing up adoringly at him. How lucky could a man get?

"OK, Dr Cathy, what would you like me to do first?"

"Go and call the next patient in, please."

"Do you have a list?"

She gave him a wry grin. "A list? Now, there's a novel idea. If you stand in the doorway, the patients will have decided who's next."

CHAPTER EIGHT

YANNIS parked the car in the drive at the front of the house and switched off the engine.

For a few moments they both sat completely still, relishing the peace and quiet of their idyllic surroundings after the noise and non-stop demands of the day.

Yannis turned to look at Cathy, sitting so still with a shaft of moonlight shining through the open car window onto her beautiful face. Cathy turned her head and saw he'd been studying her profile. For an awful moment she wondered if the loving look on his face was really for her.

No! She mustn't think like that! And she must also remember that she wasn't committing herself to a relationship. This was one romantic night together, not looking into the future. No strings attached.

He leaned across and took hold of her hand. "What's the matter? What's troubling you, Cathy? Are you still worried about Daniella? I've told you, she's in good hands up there in Obstetrics. Tomorrow, I'll get in touch with her mother, ask her to come in and see me, explain the situation and take it from there. I'll get in touch with Social Services as well but I'll take the first step to resolving the situation."

Relief flooded through her—on both levels, professional and personal. He was a fantastic doctor who really cared about all his patients. An honest, caring, wonderful man. How could she possibly continue to doubt whether he would stay with her if she were to commit to a meaningful relationship? She couldn't walk away from everything that was building up between them. Her feelings for this man were deepening in spite of the fears that had grown out of her past experiences, especially with Dave.

"I'm tired, that's all," she said quietly. "It's been a long day."

He gave her a relieved smile. For one awful moment he'd felt she might be having regrets about coming home with him. Last time she'd spent the night here he'd put her in the guest room. He'd spent the night aware of how near she'd been but afraid to spoil their early tenuous friendship. But they'd moved on now and tonight she would be with him, in his bed.

He drew her into his arms. "Let me take you inside and take care of you. You need to relax now. I'll open a bottle of champagne to celebrate."

She looked up into his dark brown searching eyes. "What are we celebrating?"

"The end of the day, the moon, the stars, Rose's birthday, the joy of being together… Come inside and let's get on with the celebrations."

His arm was around her waist as they went into the large entrance hall. The house was still and quiet but Eleni had left lights on to welcome them. There was a piece of paper on the kitchen table instructing Yannis what she'd prepared for their supper.

Cathy sank down on the old wooden armchair beside the wide iron stove and watched Yannis as he opened the champagne he'd taken out of the fridge. Bubbles ran down the side of the glass as he handed it to her.

He moved to the other side of the fireplace, sitting down in the other almost identical chair. Glancing across at Cathy, he felt relieved that she seemed to be gathering her strength again. He cared so much for her now that he couldn't bear to see her looking worried. She was becoming central to his life and he wanted so much to think that she would always be with him. But always was a long time and so much happened along the paths they were both treading, sometimes together, sometimes apart.

He raised his glass. "Here's to us!"

She smiled at his jocular tone. He must be just as physically tired as she was but he was making the effort to appear relaxed and refreshed.

"I'll drink to that!"

She raised her glass to his.

"I brought these chairs over from the house where I was born," Yannis told her. "When I sold the house I put some of the furniture in storage. As soon as I was settled in here, I reclaimed it. There are various pieces dotted all over the house."

"It's good to have memories from the past around you."

"I remember my grandmother sitting in this chair. I think I must have been about six or seven when I listened to her giving my mother a lecture on how my father wasn't good enough for her. My mother! My father! The two people I loved most in all the world."

"Did your grandmother know you were listening in?"

"Not exactly. My mother had sent me out of the room when her mother had started ranting at her. I went out but I stayed the other side of the door and heard everything. Apparently, my grandmother hadn't wanted my mother to marry my father because she didn't trust him to stay faithful. She'd thought he would leave her once I was born. I think she must have been pregnant with me when they got married."

"But your father stayed with your mother till he died, didn't he?"

"Oh, they were really happy, so in love as far as I remember. When I heard my grandmother shouting at my mother I wanted to go back and stick up for her."

He leaned his head against the back of the chair and looked up at the high ceiling. "Strange how memories come flooding back once you trigger them off. Do you find that?"

She nodded. "Often. Happy memories, unhappy memories. Once you set them off they won't stop coming. My mother made the best of everything but it was difficult for her to be left alone to bring me up by herself."

He brought the champagne bottle across and topped up her glass. "Did you have any idea that your father was going to leave your mother?"

"Oh, yes! He often went out and didn't come back for a few days. When he actually went away for good I kept expecting him to come back, but he never did."

"How awful for you!"

"Not really. I'd got used to having my mother to myself. I don't think she missed him either. She missed the small amounts of money he gave towards the housekeeping but that was all."

She broke off, not wanting to dwell any more on the hard times in her past. Was the possibility of real happiness with a good man beckoning her? Could she trust her own judgement? Even if she decided to trust Yannis completely, there was still the permanent presence of the iconic first wife to contend with.

She'd seen the photographs everywhere she'd gone. A beautiful young woman who would stay forever young, forever faultless. Her long dark hair always looked as if it had been styled professionally. Her mouth with the impeccable pearly white teeth smiling at the camera. The beautiful eyes showing such love towards the photographer—which of course, must have been Yannis.

Don't dwell on it, she told herself once more.

She put down her champagne glass on the small table beside her. "You know, every family seems to have its problems. It's how you deal with them that matters. I remember my mother telling me that if something needs changing, you should have the courage to change it. If there's something that you have to put up with, stop moaning and put up with it. But make sure you know the difference between the two situations and act accordingly."

"Wise woman, your mother. Rather like you."

"I'm not wise! I try to learn by my mistakes and..." She broke off, telling herself it was time to lighten the conversation. "What's that wonderful cooking smell that's getting my taste buds excited?"

Yannis laughed and picked up the oven glove from the side of the stove. "According to her note, I think it's Eleni's famous beef cooked in Metaxas brandy."

He opened the oven door and the delicious

aroma wafted across towards Cathy. "Mmm. If that tastes half as good as it smells…"

He led her into the dining room and held out a chair before lighting the candelabrum. Returning from the kitchen moments later, he placed the casserole on the table.

She discovered how hungry she was when she took her first mouthful of the delicious dish.

"Mmm. That's absolute heaven. I'm so glad you invited me to your dinner party this evening, Dr Yannis."

Stretching out her hand, she reached across the table to grasp his.

He smiled happily. "I'm glad you were free this evening."

"Oh, I was just having a quiet time to keep myself amused. Delivering a baby, comforting a distraught teenage mum, you know the sort of thing."

"Absolutely! All in a day's work."

She took another mouthful as she watched Yannis opening a bottle of red wine.

"I have to say this is one of my favourite restaurants in the whole of the Greek islands."

"Mine too."

He leaned over her, his hand caressing the back

of her shoulders as he poured some wine into her glass.

"I feel strong enough to go back and help the poor night staff, Yannis."

He gave her a wry grin as he sat down again. "Steady on! The poor night staff haven't worked all day. Besides, I need you here so you're not going anywhere. Don't get any ideas about leaving me alone tonight."

"That suits me fine. It's good to be needed."

He swallowed hard as he looked at the beautiful woman across the table from him. He'd been so lucky to have known two perfect women in his life.

Cathy recognised the gleam in his eye and held her breath. His expression was exactly the same as when he'd looked across the table in the cabin of the boat. She sensed instinctively that he was thinking about Maroula.

At the present moment she was feeling happy to be spending an evening like this with this wonderful man. She wasn't going to dwell on the problems of their relationship. Tonight was all that mattered. She would just imagine there had been no yesterday, there was no tomorrow, that only the present mattered.

She smiled as she put down her fork on the empty plate. "That was utterly delicious. Eleni did us proud tonight. Where do you get your mushrooms?"

"Petros brings them from the field behind their house. And the rest of the vegetables come from the kitchen garden here, potatoes, beans, peppers, courgettes. I've never been so spoilt in all my life."

He hesitated. "You know, I feel as if I shouldn't have said that. It somehow reflects badly on Maroula's cooking. She could cook…but…well, not like this."

Cathy remained very still as she watched Yannis frowning. At least the goddess Maroula had been as human as she was!

She allowed her wineglass to be topped up, revelling in the closeness of the wine waiter as he deliberately lingered beside her. She felt utterly replete now and certainly relaxed enough to look forward to the night ahead. When she'd first arrived she'd felt she could have fallen asleep in the car. But now…!

Now she was ready for anything. Maybe it was the champagne, red wine and delicious food. Or perhaps it was spending time with a man she simply enjoyed being with, a man who made her feel relaxed, content and safe. Simply sitting by the fireside, reminiscing about family and past times, good and bad. Being able to say anything she wanted, knowing that Yannis would listen and understand.

She didn't want to change anything about him at all—even if she could. She realised she'd never felt like this about any man in her life before.

He leaned forward. "You're looking very serious. Is something the matter?"

She shook her head. "Everything is…perfect."

He put down the wine bottle and drew her to her feet, enclosing her in his strong, muscular arms.

"I'll bring coffee upstairs…later."

"Good idea." She gazed up at him, unable to get enough of the adoring expression in his eyes.

He turned away for a moment to blow out the candles. Then, before she knew what was happening, he'd swept her up into his arms and was carrying her out towards the wide staircase.

He laid her down on the bed, his fingers deftly undoing the buttons on her blouse. She reached up, desperate to feel his skin against hers.

When they were both naked he lifted her again

and carried her into the bathroom. She was barely aware of the opulent surroundings as she stepped into the scented bath he was preparing, revelling in the swish of the water around her body as she sank back against the fragrant foam.

He climbed in beside her and they lay together in a spoon shaped embrace, the contact of skin against skin driving them both wild with anticipation. Then he turned her over to face him and tantalised her body, with his fingers dwelling just long enough in the places where her anticipation was at its highest level.

"Yannis," she moaned as the sensual movements of his fingers became more than she could take. She was now desperate for the ultimate consummation. As she moulded herself against him he thrust inside her, his muscles quivering against her until they became one complete rhythmic body fused in an orgasmic frenzy.

She cried out over and over again as she found herself in an experience so completely unworldly she felt she was floating somewhere in outer space on an ethereal cloud.

For what seemed like an infinity they lay together in this climactic fusion until Yannis moved to one side and put an arm around her quivering shoulders.

She lay back against him and looked up at the tiled ceiling above her. It was only then that she realised how enormous this bath really was.

"Is this a jacuzzi?" she murmured, not wanting to move away from the comfort of Yannis's arms.

"Mmm," he whispered. "Shall I turn it on?"

"Do I have to move?" she asked languidly.

"Absolutely not."

She felt him putting out an arm to flick a switch and then bringing it back to complete their embrace again. She was conscious of the gentle vibration of the water soothing her satiated body.

"Mmm, that's nice. Do you lie in your jacuzzi every night like this?"

"Only when I can catch a mermaid to share it with me. I spotted you in the sea this afternoon and I thought to myself, She'll be okay for tonight."

"Only okay?"

"Actually, much better than I could ever have imagined," he whispered as his lips came down on hers.

She felt her body quivering again, synchronising

with the movement of the water as she gave herself up to the continued heaven of their joint passion.

Someone was stroking her wet skin. She was waking up in the strangest place. Had she fallen asleep in the sea? Oh, no. "Rose!"

"Darling, Rose isn't here with us!"

Strong arms were holding her safe as she came back through the haze of her sleep-befuddled brain.

"Yannis! Oh, thank heaven it's you. I thought I was swimming with Rose." She looked around her at the enormous jacuzzi. "How long have I been asleep?"

"Only a few minutes. It seemed a pity to wake you, so I switched off the jacuzzi and cradled you in my arms. I was almost asleep myself when you woke up just now."

He gave her a sexy grin. "Actually, I'd sort of decided to wake you." He leaned forward and placed his lips gently on hers.

"Let's dry off and go to bed," he whispered against her lips.

The next time she awoke she could see the early-morning light stealing through the French windows. Half-remembered visions of last night were jumbled together in her drowsy mind. Yannis was always centre stage in every vision.

What a man! It had been a night to remember, a memory nothing and nobody could ever take away from her in the future, whatever it might hold.

She leaned her head back on the pillow as a niggle of self-doubt tried to impose itself into her brain. How would she feel when the sexual euphoria had evaporated and she had to face the cold dawn of reality?

She crept out of bed, planning to sit on the balcony so that she could watch the sunrise. Through the window she could see the haze hanging over the water and a red glow appearing along the top of the hill opposite the house.

As she moved, she heard Yannis stirring. He reached out towards her just as she was slipping her feet down to the soft lamb's-wool rug at the side of the bed.

"You're not leaving, are you?"

She heard the urgency in his voice. Part of him was joking and yet the insecurity surrounding him was palpable.

She turned and sat down on the edge of the bed. "I'm going to watch the sunrise."

"I'll come with you."

They were just in time to see the tiny triangle of light peeping out from a cleft in the peak at the top of the hill. Slowly at first and then gathering momentum the round ball of the sun revealed itself in its full morning glory.

"Magic!" she breathed. "Every time I see a sunrise or a sunset it never ceases to amaze me."

"And what a wonderful night we've had," he said huskily, drawing her closer to him.

They stood entwined in their embrace, naked skin against naked skin, in the warming rays of the sun.

"We're like Adam and Eve at the dawning of time," Cathy said, as she pulled herself gently away from his arms. "Time to leave paradise."

"Let's stay longer in paradise before we go back to the real world. I'll get you a robe. The sun is warming up but it's still a bit chilly for you."

"Thanks." He put the fluffy white towelling robe around her shoulders and she slipped into it.

He moved a couple of cushioned wicker chairs

to the front of the balcony. "Would you like that coffee now?"

She smiled. "You mean the after-supper coffee you promised to bring upstairs last night?"

He grinned. "I did say later, didn't I? Although I hadn't intended it to be breakfast time."

"I'm not complaining."

She sat very still on the balcony, snuggling into Yannis's enormous robe. The haze on the water hung over parts of the garden as well. The grass that she could see was covered in dew. Somewhere in one of the trees a bird was singing its welcome to the dawn. The same rhythmic repetition she'd heard birds use in England.

He returned carrying a large tray and placed it on the wooden table at the edge of the balcony.

"Toast, apricot jam, fruit, coffee, orange juice. Is there anything else we might need?"

"We've got absolutely everything. I'm starving."

Yannis smiled. "Can't think why!"

She noticed he was wearing a beach towel slung round his waist. It showed off his muscular, athletic legs to perfection, she thought. She was glad he'd given her his robe. It would be a pity to deny her such a stimulating artistic vision to appreciate during breakfast.

Whereas she wasn't so sure what she would look like if she was simply wrapped round with a towel. And she desperately needed a shower—by herself!

Yannis's mobile was making itself heard from the bedroom. He went inside.

"Yes, Sister... No, that's OK. I'm always awake at this early hour."

Cathy smiled at him through the open doors. He pulled a face to indicate it was work he could do without.

He sat down again and picked up a piece of toast.

"Night Sister would like me to get in before she goes off duty this morning. She wasn't happy with the diagnosis that the house surgeon gave her just now for one of her newly admitted female patients. I've told her to starve the patient and I'll take her down to Theatre as soon as I get in. From the symptoms she just described she could be right in her diagnosis of an ectopic pregnancy."

"Is the alternative diagnosis appendicitis?"

Yannis nodded, still chewing thoughtfully.

"It's not an uncommon mistake," Cathy said.

"But presumably the house surgeon has ordered the tests that reveal the correct diagnosis."

"Yes. Night Sister wants me to check the results as soon as I get in. Which I think should be a few minutes from now." He was standing up. "They're sending a hospital car to collect me. I'll ask Petros to drive you home later... No, don't rush. Take your time. Eleni will be in this morning to clear up the mess we left downstairs so just spend your time getting ready."

She heard the car in the drive, peeped over the balcony and watched him being driven away. She was queen of the castle now—and what a castle! As she padded over the thick carpet towards the bathroom she paused beside the photograph on the table near the window. Another photo of Maroula she hadn't seen! They were everywhere in the house.

She blocked off her uncharitable thoughts as soon as they arose. It didn't do to dwell on them. Moving swiftly over to the bed, she picked up her mobile from the bedside table. She'd kept it switched on all night but Anna had obviously not felt the need to call her.

As she placed her phone on the table beside the shower cubicle, she reflected that it was far too early to call Anna. She had time to take that much-needed shower she'd been promising herself.

Arriving at the hospital, she had a feeling of déjà vu when the receptionist told her that Dr Karavolis would like to see her when she got in. Apparently, he was in Theatre.

She hurried up, taking the lift, standing to one side so that a porter could bring in a pre-operative patient.

She went into the theatre anteroom. Yannis was peeling off his gloves at the sink. He turned round.

"We were right. It was an ectopic. In the left Fallopian tube. I had to excise it but the other one seems viable and the patient is young and otherwise healthy. So a future pregnancy should be possible."

He walked across and stood looking down at her with the confident assurance of someone who felt at ease in their relationship. He was standing very close to her now, but moved back as the swing door into Theatre opened.

"Sister, you'll get those biopsies and tests on the

viable Fallopian tube done as soon as possible, won't you?"

"Of course, sir." Theatre Sister went out into the corridor.

"So was everything OK at home when you left?"

"Yes, Eleni is already bustling around clearing up and cleaning. What a treasure!"

"And how was your treasure when you went up home?"

"Do you mean Rose or Anna?"

He smiled. "Rose, actually."

"Happy to see me and equally happy to carry on playing with the other children in the house." She paused. "About her birthday party…"

"Yes?"

"Anna was rather hoping to be involved."

He smiled. "But of course she must be involved. I'll arrange to have everybody brought to my house. Anna, her grandchildren and their friends, the more the merrier, don't you think?"

All things were possible with Yannis when he was in a mood like this. The night they'd spent together seemed to have given him new energy.

She just hoped he wouldn't be plagued with guilt when he returned home this evening and went up to his room alone. Would he pick up that photograph from the table and...?

"Cathy, what's the matter?"

He put his hands on her arms and looked down into her eyes.

"Nothing! Just thinking about the day ahead. I'll go up to Obstetrics and check on Daniella and Ariadne."

He drew her towards him and held her close for a few moments before releasing her so that he could look deep into her eyes.

"You would tell me if there was a problem, wouldn't you?"

She nodded. "I haven't got a problem and, yes, I would tell you."

She moved out of the circle of his arms and hurried away before she could say anything more.

As she went along the corridor she could feel herself coming back down to earth. She'd had her wonderful night with Yannis. Now she must face reality. Their problems were still with them. Yannis's obsession with his beloved wife, his guilt at betraying her memory. Her own fear of committing herself to a meaningful relationship with any man, however sincere he appeared. The real crux of the matter was that she didn't believe she would be enough for Yannis, like she hadn't been enough for Dave, like her mother hadn't been enough for her father.

Was history repeating itself?

CHAPTER NINE

CATHY found Ariadne propped up against her pillows feeding both her newborn twins. With the practised ease of a mother of five, the twins hadn't fazed her. She'd tucked their legs under her arms, allowing them to suckle at her breasts. She smiled with delight when Cathy walked in.

"Cathy! I was hoping you would come in to see me this morning. How was your night over at Nimborio with Yannis?"

Cathy smiled. Ariadne had become a personal friend over the weeks she'd been caring for her. She'd trained as a nurse in England and had spent time as an au pair with an English family before she'd married. So her English was excellent and they usually conversed in that language. But Cathy was usually careful how much she divulged of her personal life. She'd been tired last night when she'd called in to check on her and had probably given away too much information.

"Listen, Ariadne, you positively dragged out

of me the fact that I was going out for supper at Yannis's house. What makes you think supper lasted all night?"

Ariadne deftly swapped her twins over so that each could take a different breast. "It's just the way you look this morning. Sort of radiant... in a shattered sort of way. I may be a long-time married woman but I do remember that feeling. Mmm, lucky you! Correct me if I'm wrong, but it's obvious that Yannis adores you."

"Ariadne, I prefer to talk about you and how you're feeling, not about my private love life," Cathy said, trying to look serious and professional but still unable to keep that wonderful warm glow to herself.

At least with her other patients she wouldn't have to submit to the third degree!

Ariadne laughed. "Aha! So you admit you're having a love life?"

Cathy smiled. "No comment! I'm here to check you out, not the other way round. I've got to make out a report so..."

"Oh, that young obstetrician came in earlier. The one who looks as if he's just left school but seems to know everything about babies. He gave me a complete examination and put it straight on the computer thing he always carries with him. It's all there for the medical staff to read."

"In that case, why did I come in to see you this morning?"

Ariadne took one hand off her boy twin and patted the side of her bed.

"To have a girly chat, I hope. Can't you see how bored I'm getting in here? These little darlings, although very precious to me, are numbers four and five in my family. Demetrius is always off on business somewhere, trying to keep the wolf from the door of our large family, so I need some intellectual stimulation from time to time."

Cathy sat down on the side of the bed. "I don't know about intellectual but I suppose it's my duty to spend time with a patient who's had a rough time."

"Oh, it wasn't that rough. You and Yannis were wonderful with me. We must keep in touch after you let me out of here. Then I can see if the pair of you have the sense to make a go of it."

Cathy raised an eyebrow. "We're at the stage where it could go either way. You know, of course, his first wife died?"

"Yes, everybody heard about that soon after he came here, but nobody likes to talk about it. He seemed so sad when he first arrived on the island but you've certainly brought him out of his shell. So what's the problem? My Demetrius has a first wife. He was divorced when we first met and look how happy we are now. His first marriage only lasted a couple of years before he found her in bed with his best friend. He's had no contact with her since. His solicitors dealt with the divorce. He can't stand the sound of her name!"

"Well, that's slightly different to our situation," Cathy said quietly.

Ariadne frowned. "You've lost me."

Cathy took a deep breath. "Yannis still adores his wife."

"His deceased wife?"

"Yes, they were idyllically happy apparently and he still loves her."

They both remained silent. Only the sound of the suckling babies disturbed the peace and calm of the private room. Ariadne spoke first to break the awkward silence.

"I can see what you're up against now."

Cathy took a deep breath. "And there's also the fact that he feels guilty when…when we're together, enjoying ourselves."

"Like last night?"

"I don't know about last night. It was…yes, it was fabulous, but I don't think he's had time to worry about it yet. Actually…"

The door opened and Yannis came in, his theatre mask slung underneath his chin.

He smiled. "Don't let me stop your little chat, ladies. I presume Cathy is telling you how to take care of your newborn babies?"

Ariadne grinned cheekily. "Invaluable advice, Yannis, but I'm glad you came to answer a few important questions, like—"

"I was just telling Ariadne we were having a birthday party for Rose and I wondered if she and Demetrius could come along, bringing all the children, of course."

"Yes, that's right." Ariadne said, quickly recognising she might make things worse if she tried to interfere with their love life. "I've agreed to check diaries with the boss when he comes in. Where did you say you were holding the party, Cathy?"

"Over at my place," Yannis filled in, wondering why the two women were looking so secretive. "You should be fine by then. Your obstetrician has given me a full report on your condition. I came to say that we think we could let you go home tomorrow if you've managed to arrange for full-time help at home."

"Don't worry about that. It's all taken care of. My mother has moved in temporarily and we're already employing a full-time nurse. I shall be spoiled rotten when I get home. That's not to say I wouldn't like the occasional house call from the pair of you."

Yannis smiled. "We'll see what we can do."

He turned to look at Cathy. "Have you been along to see Daniella yet? She was asking for you earlier."

"She's next on my list."

"OK. Let me know what you arrange with Social Services. I'll see you later."

"He's obviously in a hurry to get back to Theatre," Cathy said, taking the little girl twin who'd now stopped suckling and putting her over her shoulder to release the wind that was bothering her.

"Oh, he's perfect for you," Ariadne said dreamily. "Don't let him slip through your fingers."

"Everything we've said was in confidence," Cathy said quickly.

"Of course it was. Anyway, you didn't tell me anything I didn't know about...except the fact that he's hanging onto his memories. That's a tricky one, but I do wish you both the best of luck. It's obvious there is something between you."

"Thanks." The baby she was holding gave a loud burp. "Good girl! When are you going to give names to your twins?"

"As soon as I can nail my husband down to spending a couple of hours with me. Time is always a problem with him. But we'll get there. I might even persuade him to cancel everything and come to Rose's birthday party."

"Yes, do. Yannis would like some male support amongst all the mothers, grandmothers and children.

"He adores Rose, doesn't he?"

Cathy nodded. "It's almost as if…well, he's almost paternal with her. And she adores him."

"And so do you, so go for it."

The door opened and Obstetrics Sister came in. "Oh, Dr Cathy, I came to find you. I heard you were in here."

"I'm just going, Sister." Cathy finished changing the baby's nappy and laid her down in one of the cribs at the side of the bed.

"Could you go and see Daniella, please? She's been asking for you."

Sister drew her on one side. "Dr Karavolis contacted Social Services this morning but they can't send anyone in today and the poor girl is worrying too much about what her mother will do when she hears from them." She hesitated. "I actually know the family and I could perhaps ease the situation myself."

"That would be a big help if you could, Sister."

"If you'd like to come into my office we can discuss the situation."

"Daniella's mother is a neighbour of mine," Sister said as soon as they were alone in her office. "I've known Daniella since she was a small child. Her mother's had a hard time with her husband, Daniella's father. He left her last year and went off to Rhodes to live with someone a lot younger than himself. Daniella's a hot-headed individual—a bit like her father—and she kept on having rows with her mother. In the end she simply upped and left. Next thing we heard was that she was living with her father and his girlfriend on Rhodes."

"So her mother didn't turn her out, as she told me?"

"Maria's a good mother. She's bringing up six

children on her own. Daniella's the eldest. She'll give her a good talking-to when she knows her predicament but she'll welcome her back—and the new baby. I know she will. Shall I phone her and ask her to come in?"

"I think that could well be the answer to the problem," Cathy said thoughtfully. "Thank you very much, Sister. I'll go and see her now and prepare her for the fact that she's soon going to see her mother. From what she said last night, she may not be too pleased about that."

"I'm sure it's for the best, Doctor."

"Let's hope so."

'So how are you feeling now, Daniella?" Cathy looked down at the sullen young girl stretched out on top of her bed. "I heard you wanted to see me."

"Yes, well, nobody else around here seems to know what to do with me. I need to see if I can go into a hostel or something till I'm feeling a bit stronger. Feel really tired today."

"That's understandable, Daniella."

Cathy pulled up a chair and sat down at the side of the bed. "We're going to keep you in here until we've sorted where you're going to live. I thought it would be best if we let your mother know you're in here and—"

"No, she'll kill me!"

"I'm sure she won't, Daniella. I'll stay with you while she's here."

"She's coming here?"

"Yes, Sister is phoning her now so it shouldn't take long for her to arrive. I understand your house is close by."

"Yes, but she'll have to get somebody to mind the kids and…"

"Yes, Sister?" Cathy looked up enquiringly.

"I've phoned your mother, Daniella, and she's on her way."

"Always poking your nose in," Daniella said under her breath.

"What was that?"

"Nothing, Sister."

"Now, I hope you're going to behave yourself when your mother comes in," Sister said. "I remember you since you were very small and you've always been difficult to handle. But just for once, can you please listen to what your mother has to say? She's been a good mother to you and she needs some respect from you, if nothing else."

"Do you understand, Daniella?" Cathy asked, firmly but kindly, as Sister left them.

She felt so sorry for her patient who, it seemed, had stood little chance in life. But at the same time she would have to grow up quickly and toe the line for the sake of this new life she'd brought into the world and also for her poor long-suffering mother.

Cathy leaned over the crib. The new baby boy's eyes were open and he appeared to be looking around as if wondering what kind of world he'd landed up in. She leaned down, picked him up into her arms and held him against her, relishing the sweet scent of freshly bathed baby, baby powder and cream.

"Who bathed your baby this morning?"

"I did." The sullen expression softened. "I've been bathing my brothers and sisters for ages, ever since I can remember, really. My mother gets so tired, she just likes to sit at the end of the day so I have to get them all ready for bed. And they stink if I put them down dirty. We've only got one bedroom with two double beds in it so we're all squashed up together. Mum sleeps downstairs so she can get a bit of peace."

Cathy felt a wave of compassion sweeping over

her. No wonder Daniella had left home. This was one family that definitely needed rehousing and to be given more help.

She looked down at this feisty young mother and hoped she could make a difference to the difficult situation. "You've got a fine son here, Daniella. He's gorgeous, your little boy. Have you got a name for him yet?"

"I thought I might call him after my dad, Elias."

"That's a good name. Your dad would like that."

"Do you think so?"

Sister came in, bringing a visitor. A small plump woman wearing a large flower-patterned apron over her long brown dress that reached almost to her ankles stood near the bedside, staring across at her daughter. She was breathing heavily, as if she'd been hurrying too fast.

Daniella pulled herself up and sat very still, watching her mother.

Cathy was feeling desperately apprehensive as she watched the tense, as yet silent confrontation. She took a deep breath, knowing she would have to act as mediator before the confrontation turned verbal or even physical.

But just as she was about to intervene, Daniella's mother moved quickly over to the bed and put her arms around her daughter. "You naughty, naughty girl! I've been so worried about you. God be praised he's answered my prayers and you've come back home!"

Relief flooded through Cathy as she watched the tears of mother and daughter mingling together as they clung to each other.

Sister touched Cathy's arm and whispered, "They're going to be all right now, Cathy."

Cathy nodded. "I'll arrange as much help for this family as I can."

Cathy looked out of the window of the tiny office she'd been given and noticed the shadows lengthening down by the harbour. Glancing at the clock, she saw she should have been off duty an hour ago. She switched off her computer with a sense of relief. It had been a busy day, as usual, but a satisfying one.

She'd had a long talk with Social Services, who were going to take over the case of Daniella's family and make sure they had as much help as possible with housing and child care. Apparently, the family network on Ceres, which had been the norm until recently, sometimes broke down.

Daniella's parents had lived on Rhodes before they'd set up house on Ceres. There were no near relatives on the island to help out and now that the father had decamped, the situation had worsened.

But as she looked out of the window at the warm friendly atmosphere down in the harbour Cathy was sure that things could only improve from now on for Daniella's family.

She went along the corridor to tell Yannis she was going off duty. He stood and came round his desk when she walked in.

"I'm just off, Yannis."

"Time for a drink?"

She shook her head. "No, I want to spend some time with Rose. I'm planning she should sleep in her own cot at home with me tonight."

"So I'll be all on my own tonight?" He drew her into his arms.

She heard his wistful tone as she allowed herself to lean against him. "I'm afraid so."

She hesitated for a moment. Ariadne's advice was at the back of her mind, urging her to go for it. But she needed to spend some real quality time with her daughter. If she invited Yannis back to her place, her loyalties would be divided. He wasn't the only one to suffer from a guilt complex!

She looked up into his dark brown eyes. "Being a working mum isn't easy, Yannis. I need to spend time alone with Rose— for both our sakes. We need to strengthen the bond between mother and daughter."

"Of course you do," he said gently, holding her even more closely.

She relaxed against him, tempted to give in to her sensual demands but held back by some inner voice warning her about becoming too complacent.

"It was when I saw Daniella and her mother today, hugging each other in spite of all they'd been through, that I realised I mustn't take my relationship with Rose for granted."

"I don't think you'll ever do that," he said.

He bent his head and kissed her gently. "Last night was wonderful," he whispered.

"Mmm." For a brief moment she snuggled against him, before making a determined effort to move from his embrace.

She had an awful feeling of déjà vu. She'd been here before, hadn't she? Given all her love to a man she'd adored, trusted completely. But he'd betrayed her. Her mother had been betrayed in the same way. Having loved her father, given him a daughter, he'd chosen to take off and leave her.

From the experiences of life she'd had so far she couldn't expect Yannis to be any different, even if he seemed completely perfect now. She'd known him such a short time, but long enough to know that he still loved his wife and there was no way he was ever going to forget the wonderful marriage they'd had. However wonderful her relationship with Yannis felt at the moment, it could crumble away when she least expected it.

But her love for Rose would always be there. Blood was thicker than water. Whatever happened in the future, the bond with her daughter would always be there and she had to continue to strengthen it. For her own sake and for Rose's.

They would need each other for the rest of their lives, no matter what happened in the future.

Yannis was looking down at her with a quizzical expression. "Cathy, I wish you'd tell me what's worrying you so deeply, something you haven't explained to me. You've hardly told me anything about the man who left you. Rose's father. Don't you think it would help if you opened up more and we could discuss it together? I could help you as you've helped me. But not until you explain what—"

"I don't want to discuss it!" She stared up into his dark brown eyes. "My past is so…so complicated and…"

"But if we could talk about together I'm sure it would help! I hate it when you draw away from and start worrying about something that I'm sure I could help you with if only you'd bring it out into the open."

He reached forward and drew her against him. She leaned against him for a few moments before pulling away again.

"I'm sorry, Yannis. I really don't want to talk about it. I'm…I'm not ready to explain. Maybe one day you'll understand why… Look, I've got to go."

CHAPTER TEN

"HAPPY birthday, dear Rose, happy birthday to you!"

Cathy was feeling complete, surrounded by people she loved—Rose, Yannis, Anna. Life was so good at the moment—but how long would this last? Was it just an illusion? Yannis hadn't made them any promises, and as time was passing she ought to make a decision before it was too late and her heart was broken, and Rose's too.

"Mama!"

Cathy smiled as she bent over her daughter.

"Blow out the candle, Rose," she said gently.

Rose looked up at her mummy enquiringly, not sure what was expected of her now.

"Look, like this," Yannis said gently, making a blowing sound and pointing to the candles on top of the cake that Eleni had gone to so much trouble to make.

He was feeling so relieved that Rose's birthday celebrations were going so well. Maybe Cathy would begin to relax soon. He hoped so because she'd seemed a bit strained for the past few days. He'd no idea what the problem was but something was definitely worrying her. Perhaps he could find out what was the matter tonight, if he could only persuade her to stay over when everyone else had gone.

Little Rose was looking up at him now, still confused about what was expected of her.

"Rose, darling," he said, bending over her as he pointed to the all-important candle. "I know you've never had a birthday before but you'll soon get used to having them. You'll get more than you need as time goes on."

Everybody laughed and Rose giggled.

"Rose, blow when I blow, OK?" He pouted his lips forward and blew gently at the edge of the table.

Rose giggled again and copied what Yannis was doing with his lips.

"Do that again," Cathy said, "but make it like that strong wind we sometimes have by the sea."

Hmm. Strong wind? OK, if that was what they all wanted. So long as she got some cake at the end of all this! Rose pouted her lips and instinctively drew in her breath to make a really big strong wind that would blow that candle thingy off the top of the cake.

Everybody was cheering now. Rose clapped her hands together like they were all doing.

"Would you like some cake, Rose?" Cathy asked her daughter.

She removed the smouldering candle and picked up the cake knife, putting her hand over Rose's and guiding her tiny fingers carefully towards the centre of the cake.

"Let's put the knife in here, Rose," Cathy said gently. "Don't worry, Yannis, I'm holding the knife very firmly. It's quite safe."

There was more clapping as Cathy guided the knife that was being loosely held by her daughter's tiny fingers into the cake.

Yannis could feel himself becoming completely sentimental as he watched Cathy and Rose reacting to each other. After Maroula had died he'd never imagined he could be so happy again. Did he deserve all this? Why couldn't he get rid of the feelings of guilt when he enjoyed himself?

"I'll take the cake to the kitchen and let Eleni cut it up with a big sharp knife," he said.

"Good idea," Cathy said.

He picked up the cake and knife and went across the lawn to the kitchen. If only he could completely commit himself to this wonderful surrogate family, deal with the guilt he felt at being so happy, and find out what it was that was troubling Cathy, life would be perfect!

"Is something worrying you, Yannis?" Cathy said, as she cradled the sleeping Rose in her arms.

"I'm fine, but I'm worried about you. I wish you'd tell me what's troubling you," he said, quietly, as he leaned over to hand her a glass of chilled champagne.

She looked up at him as she put the glass to lips. "It's been a fabulous party. Thank you so much for everything you did to make it such a success."

"It's not speeches I want, Cathy," he said evenly, pulling up a chair so that they could be close. "You haven't answered my question."

"I'm not sure how to explain it." She put down her glass on the table and looked around her at the debris left behind after the guests had gone home. Eleni and Petros were in the kitchen, putting away food, washing dishes, but they would be out here soon to clear up.

"Start by telling me what's worrying you. You've been so…preoccupied with your own thoughts for the past couple of weeks, since you stayed here that night and everything between us was so wonderful. You've kept yourself to yourself…almost as if you don't trust me any more."

"I do trust you," she told him adamantly, wanting desperately to believe what she was saying.

Of all the men she'd known in her life there had never been anyone like him. But there was always that nagging voice at the back of her mind telling her that she would never be able to hold onto him, that he would break her heart in the end. He would leave her, as her father had left her mother, as Daniella's father had left Daniella's mother. And like men in so many films she'd seen and books she'd read. It was in their nature. They were simply doing what came naturally. The grass always looked greener on the other side or, in Yannis's case, she suspected his past life when he'd been totally committed to Maroula always seemed perfect.

She remembered how she'd thought her relationship with Dave was going to last for ever but he'd decided to stay with his wife.

When this idyllic period of their life together

began to wane, would Yannis's guilt at betraying his perfect wife take over? Would he choose to go back into his safe state of bachelorhood, content to dwell on the idyllic past he'd shared with the first love of his life?

He leaned forward, putting his arms around both of them. "You mean the world to me," he said quietly. "You and Rose. I couldn't bear to lose you."

She looked up from her sleeping child into his trusting eyes. How could she doubt him at a time like this, after the wonderful day they'd had together? Why didn't she stop looking into the future and simply enjoy the present?

"I couldn't bear to lose you either, Yannis," she said softly.

He gave her a relieved smile. "Well, neither of us is going anywhere. Please stay here tonight… both of you. We can put Rose to bed in the small dressing room adjoining my bedroom."

Cathy could feel herself relaxing. Yes, she had been tense today. Probably nobody had noticed it but Yannis. But now the thought of going with the flow was very appealing. What did it matter if she was deluding herself about their relationship? The present moment was all that mattered, wasn't it?

"Yes, I'd like to stay," she said quietly. "I'll take Rose upstairs and put her into her cot."

"You'll find everything you need in the dressing room but give me a shout if you need some help. I'll stay down here and help Eleni and Petros clear up."

Cathy was halfway across the lawn to the kitchen when Eleni came out.

"Are you going to put Rose in the cot in the dressing room now?" she asked in hushed tones so as not to wake the little one. "I'll come up and help you find everything."

"Yannis says there's everything I need up there."

"Of course there is. I got the little room ready myself this morning when I suggested you and Rose might like to stay here tonight."

"That was very thoughtful of you, Eleni."

"Men never think ahead, do they? Everything spur of the moment, whereas we women are always one step ahead."

Rose stirred and opened her eyes as Cathy sat down on the chair by the side of the cot.

"I brought some clean baby clothes from my

house yesterday. My grandchildren have all grown too big for them. I thought this little nightdress would fit Rose perfectly. Might still be a bit big but you don't want it too tight, do you? It's thin cotton so she won't get too hot. I remember when my own babies were small…"

Cathy listened to the soothing voice, chatting away in Greek. What a wonderful lifestyle she was having at the moment. Working at the hospital, doing a job she was trained for, skilled at and found so stimulating and satisfying. And then being able to combine that with motherhood in an environment where she got so much help and Rose was so happy.

Rose had submitted to having the cool cotton nightdress put on her before closing her eyes again and sinking contentedly against the mattress.

"I'll cover her with the sheet, Cathy," Eleni said. "It will get cooler when the sun goes down."

Cathy nodded. It was so nice to have the advice of an older woman—even if she didn't agree with it! She would pop back soon and remove the sheet if she thought it wasn't necessary. Although Eleni was more experienced than she was in caring for babies during a hot Greek summer.

"*Efharisto poli*, thank you very much, Eleni," she said as they both tiptoed out.

"*Parakalor*," Eleni replied with a smile.

They were passing through the master bedroom when Eleni paused at the table with Maroula's photo on it. She leaned down and picked it up before turning to look at Cathy.

"I dust this every day and I can't help thinking it's time Yannis put all these photos of his late wife away, don't you?"

For a brief moment Cathy didn't know how to answer. "I'm not sure…" she began cautiously. "I think Yannis finds it comforting to have these reminders of his wife around."

"Well, it's more than three years now since she died and I think it's time he moved on completely," Eleni retorted, holding the picture at arm's length. "Some days when I'm dusting I feel like gathering up the whole lot and putting them in a box."

"Oh, you mustn't do that!"

"I don't think he'd really notice. Men aren't observant about what's sitting around in the house. When he first moved in he used to be always staring at her photos. But I've noticed he never gives them a glance nowadays."

Cathy felt her spirits lifting upwards. She could have hugged Eleni for that piece of comforting information!

"Well, I think we should leave them there until Yannis decides to put them away, Eleni," Cathy said firmly. "It has to be his decision. He will know when the time is right…even if that time never arrives."

Her voice trailed away at the end of her conclusion. She could tell by Eleni's frown that she didn't agree with her.

As they went out on to the landing and began their descent of the wide staircase, Eleni continued to put forward what she thought about the situation.

"I've always told Petros that if I go first he should find himself another wife as soon as he possibly can. Men can't manage without a woman. It's not natural for them. And Yannis has got you to care for him now so why he's hanging onto those old photos I don't know. It doesn't…"

Eleni stopped in mid-sentence as she noticed Yannis standing at the bottom of the staircase, looking up towards them.

"Cathy, I was just coming to see if Rose is OK up there."

"She's fast asleep. Eleni helped me to settle her."

"*Efharisto*, Eleni. Petros is ready to go home now. We've finished clearing up."

Eleni smiled. "*Kali nichta*. Goodnight. I'll see you both in the morning."

Yannis took hold of her hand and led her across the lawn towards the garden room. "I thought we could watch the sunset from here tonight. We're directly outside Rose's room so we'll hear her if she cries."

They sat quietly, holding hands, watching the big red ball dip down behind the hill at the back of the house. They still remained there in the gathering dusk after the sunset.

"Are you hungry, Cathy? I thought I would make us some supper. You've only been grazing at the party food. I could heat up some soup from the fridge."

"I'll help you."

As they went back into the house, she was thinking about Eleni's words. She was a very wise woman who'd worked out exactly what Yannis had to do to get his life back on track. Come to think of it, so had she! But getting him to see the light was the problem.

They ate their soup sitting at the kitchen table, a Rachmaninov CD in the background. They discussed which of his works they liked best and discovered it was his second piano concerto.

"Not surprising!" Cathy said. "I think it's everybody's favourite."

"Oh, I don't know. His third symphony is another favourite of mine."

"Yes, I like that too," she conceded as the music rolled over them. "Especially the second movement."

Yannis was watching her as she listened.

"You know, it's good to be with someone who appreciates classical music. Maroula constantly changed the music when we had the radio on in the car."

"Really? What kind of music did she prefer?"

"She liked Greek folk songs...but that was all... so..."

He was staring at her with that expression he'd had on the boat when he'd almost called her Maroula. But she was becoming immune to the fact that he thought often about his late wife. At least this time he hadn't said she was a musical genius. Now, that really would have been a pain!

"You know, Cathy, I always feel I have to be careful when I'm speaking about Maroula. I don't like to criticise her because she can't answer back. But the fact that she didn't like the same kind of music as I did was often a bone of contention between us."

"Really?" She found she was holding her breath at the revelation. "That bad, was it?"

"Well, no relationship can be perfect all the time, can it?"

"Of course not."

Well, glory be! Was he beginning to see the light? Was the goddess beginning to slip from her pedestal? She stood up and began to clear the dishes.

"I'll go up and check on Rose," she said.

"I'll join you soon," he said absently, as he changed the CD. "I just want to listen to this new CD I bought last week. Mozart's piano concerto number twenty. It's a new recording by a young Greek pianist which I'd like to hear. I couldn't resist buying it. The internet just makes shopping too easy."

"I'd love to hear it but not tonight."

As she went up the stairs she reflected that the easy relationship they'd had together tonight gave her hope that progress was being made. She would be an idiot to leave all this behind just when they were beginning to really get to know one another.

She was lying in the bath when he came in dressed in his robe. He sat down on the edge of the bath.

"Shall I put the jacuzzi switch on?

"Not yet. I was just having a time of quiet contemplation."

"Thinking about what?" he asked as he slipped off his robe and joined her.

"Mainly about us."

"Mmm, that's good," he said, snuggling up to her. "I love having you here to stay with me. Maybe…"

He hesitated. He'd been going to suggest she bring Rose and move in with him, but the way she'd been behaving towards him recently meant he didn't think she would consider it a good idea. There was so much about Cathy he didn't understand. That relationship she'd had with the man who'd fathered Rose must have been difficult. What man in his right mind would abandon his girlfriend when she was pregnant? It would be a long time before Cathy was ready to put her trust in someone so that she would make any kind of commitment.

And he needed to make sure he was ready for commitment himself. He still hadn't learned to handle the guilt that nagged him constantly about liaising with a woman other than Maroula. He still had awful flashbacks in his dreams about that fateful weekend. He shouldn't have left her... not straight after their awful row...

Cathy could feel Yannis tensing up. The more she got to know him the more she felt he was holding something back. He'd told her so many intimate truths that he'd never told anyone else but there was still something secret. Something that he daren't divulge to anybody. Maybe that was why he still suffered from guilt.

"You would tell me if something was worrying you, wouldn't you, Yannis?" she whispered.

"Of course." He moved away to press the switch that set off the jacuzzi jets. "Let's have some bubbles to float away our problems."

"If only it were that simple," she said quietly as the jets came on to drown her voice.

He moved back again and took her into his

arms. The close contact of his skin, the soothing bubbles relaxed her until she found herself desperate to make love with him. The last time they'd been in here together neither of them could wait to quench their sexual longings for each other.

But tonight they took everything more slowly, savouring every step towards consummation. As she felt herself reaching orgasm she cried out, unable to control the vibrations of passion that had taken over her body. Last time had been out of this world. This time had been completely different, more cerebral, each giving more consideration to the reaction of the other as they moved forward towards their joint climax.

"You know, Yannis," she said breathlessly, as she lay back amongst the bubbles cocooned in his strong muscular arms. "Making love is different every time, isn't it?"

"I should hope so, otherwise couples who'd been together for a long time would get terribly bored."

"Do you think they would?"

"Probably. But we don't need to worry about it. We've only known each other a matter of weeks, haven't we? Which reminds me. I had a phone call from Manolis yesterday. He's been offered a promotion in the hospital in Sydney. He and Tanya are thinking of staying out there for at least another year and he wanted to know if I was interested in applying for permanent post of medical director at the hospital."

"And what did you say?" She shifted herself in his arms and moved to one of the seats in the sides of the jacuzzi.

"I said I'd think about it and let him know. He told me he'd have to advertise the post as a matter of protocol but he wanted me to know that from the reports sent back to him from the chairman of the Ceres hospital board the job would be mine if I applied."

"So what is there to think about? Don't you want to be permanent director?"

He hesitated. "I used to be too ambitious. I've been careful about each step I take since..."

He broke off, thinking once more about that fatal day. He thought he'd changed since then but deep down he was still the same. But he'd learned what was most important in his life.

Cathy was waiting for him to continue. She knew that it wasn't a good idea to enquire too deeply when Yannis was deep in thought. He was obviously thinking about something that had happened in the past. He would tell her in his own good time—or not! She was learning to be patient and fatalistic. What would be would be.

He focused his eyes directly at her as he came out of his reverie. "Are you going to apply for an extension to your contract when it expires at the end of October?"

"Hadn't thought about it yet," she lied.

Of course she'd thought about it! How could she not have? But until she knew whether Yannis wanted to commit to a more permanent relationship she wasn't going to commit herself to anything. She wasn't going to hang around for ever. Either he stopped sitting on the fence and asked her…asked her for what?

She was his number one girlfriend but that wasn't enough. Before Rose got much older she had to be careful who she allowed her daughter to regard as a father figure. And she had to make sure, this time, hat their relationship, fantastic as it was at the moment, wasn't going to collapse when the man in her life decided he wanted to renew his old lifestyle and left her in the lurch.

"Let me know when you've decided what you want to do at the end of October, Cathy."

"Of course."

She pulled herself out of the water and wrapped herself in one of the huge fluffy towels. She wouldn't make any decision until he'd made his intentions towards her clearer. Once bitten, twice shy! And she'd been bitten more than once or twice so was many times more shy than most women.

She pretended to be asleep when he climbed into bed. She found herself sleeping fitfully, turning over carefully so as not to waken him. As the dawn light began to filter in through the French doors that led to the balcony she came to the decision that she would enjoy her relationship with Yannis until her contract expired at the end of October. But then, if nothing had changed, if he was still clinging to the past, unwilling to move forward and make a permanent commitment with her, she would go back to England. She had to come to terms with things herself.

She sat alone on the balcony, watching the sun come up over the hill on the other side of the water. Yannis was still asleep or feigning sleep, she didn't know which, but she'd had time to herself to make her decision. For the last few weeks of the summer out here she was going to enjoy what they had together and not think too much about whether it was permanent or temporary.

Make the most of every day, she told herself, and don't look too far ahead. Whatever happened, she would be in control this time and well pre-pared to deal with it.

She was fixing Rose into her high chair down in the kitchen when Yannis came down.

"You shouldn't have let me sleep so long."

He flopped down into the armchair at the side of the stove, running his hands through his ruf-fled hair. She thought he looked like a truculent boy who was trying to think where he'd put his homework and her heart went out to him as she tried to stifle her longing to go back to bed and make love with him.

"Did you sleep well, Cathy?"

"Yes." She was getting good at saying what she knew he expected to hear.

She handed him a cup of coffee. He put it down on the table so that his hands were free to draw her into his arms.

"Mmm, good morning, darling," he said, as he finished kissing her.

"Mama!" Rose called in a demanding tone from the table.

Cathy went back to the table and kissed her daughter. Rose gurgled with delight and offered her mummy the piece of bread she'd half eaten.

"No, thank you, darling, I'm going to have some toast in a moment."

Yannis sat down beside Rose and kept her plate replenished with bread, honey, yoghurt and fruit.

Cathy was the first to leave the table and take some of the dishes over to the sink. She glanced at the clock.

"Time to make a move, Rose," she said, hauling her daughter out of the high chair and wiping a damp cloth around her face.

Yannis stood up and held out his arms towards Rose. She laughed with delight as Cathy handed her over.

"Rose almost walked yesterday," he told Cathy as he held the little girl against him. "I'm going to take her out onto the lawn and see how she gets on."

"I'll give her a quick shower afterwards," Cathy said, turning away to move some more dishes.

Yannis put out a hand to detain her. "Come

with us outside. We can take a few minutes to play with Rose. These early days in a baby's life are so precious, aren't they? We can't get them back again when they're gone."

She took hold of his hand and they went out on to the sunlit grass. She could hear the sound of the gentle waves lapping on the shore. He put Rose gently down on the grass and then offered her his hand. She hauled herself up, holding onto Yannis to steady herself. She took a few tentative steps and giggled with delight. Very gently, Yannis loosened his fingers from her grasp. She looked up questioningly.

"It's OK, Rose. I'm not going to leave you. And the grass is very soft if you fall."

Rose smiled, held out her arms at the sides to balance herself and staggered across the grass for a few seconds before sitting down.

"Clever girl!" Cathy said. "Come to Mummy!"

Rose looked up at Yannis, holding out her little hand for him to help her up.

As soon as he'd set her upright she started off again, staggering back across the grass unaided like a baby foal that had just been born.

"Marvellous!" Cathy said as her daughter reached her and collapsed against her. "Oh,

Yannis, I'm so glad we came out here. I'll remember this morning for…for a long time."

Her eyes locked with Yannis's in a heart-rending gaze.

She took a deep breath. Tears were prickling the back of her eyes. If only she could be sure that Yannis would be with her for the rest of her life. But she'd decided not to worry about how long their relationship was going to last, hadn't she? They'd enjoyed this precious moment together. The memory would stay with her for ever.

She turned away before and the precious moment was gone.

She took a deep breath as she composed herself. "Time to go, everybody," she said, gathering up her daughter.

CHAPTER ELEVEN

As Cathy switched off her computer at the end of another busy day at the hospital, her mind was on the phone call she'd just received. The summer weeks were flying by so quickly now. The tourists on holiday on Ceres had made the workload heavy. She was coping with her busy lifestyle, but always felt exhausted at the end of each day—like now. She'd been longing to go back to Anna's and pick up Rose so that the two of them could relax together for the evening.

But Anna's phone call just now had added to her problems. She stood up and was halfway to the door when someone knocked.

She opened the door. "Hi, Yannis. I'm just on my way out."

"You look tired. Let me take you…"

"Not tonight. I've got to go up to Anna's. She's just phoned to say she's got to go over to Rhodes tomorrow to be with her sister who's seriously ill in hospital. Her nearest relatives have been alerted and are gathering there as soon as they can make it. Anna could be there a week or two, so…"

"So you're worrying about Rose," he said, taking hold of her hand as they walked down the corridor towards the side door of the hospital.

"And Anna as well. She sounded so worried when she rang that I thought something had happened to Rose. It was almost a relief when I realised my only problem was to find child care for Rose. Of course I told her I'm terribly sorry for the distress she's going through at the moment but she assured me she's tough enough to handle it. She said she'd had enough practice in her long life to handle anything. That I can believe!"

"Has Anna got enough help with organising her transfer over to Rhodes tomorrow?"

Cathy nodded. "One of her sons is coming to take her down to the early ferry tomorrow morning. But I need to get up to take Rose off her hands as soon as possible and give her some space to get ready."

He held the outer door open for Cathy to go out first. "I've got the car with me. I'll take you up to Anna's now."

She watched his firm hands on the wheel as he steered the car through the main entrance of the hospital. The porter on the door saluted him. Yannis smiled and saluted him back. The porter grinned happily.

Over the past few weeks she'd come to realise that Yannis had become a very popular temporary director of the hospital. She wondered if she could take any credit for bringing him out of his shell. What was important was that she hoped he was going to make a decision about becoming permanent director.

"Someone to care for Rose is not going to be a problem," Yannis said evenly, as he began the steep ascent up the hillside road.

"Eleni would be delighted to take care of her. You know how she adores her. She's actually got her first great grandchild staying with her at the moment. Little Alissa is two years old and her mother, Eleni's eldest daughter, is expecting her second baby soon, so Eleni asked if she could bring Alissa to work with her sometimes so that her daughter could get some rest."

Cathy was overawed by the proposition, playing for time before she gave a definitive answer.

"It would certainly solve the problem," she said cautiously. "But Eleni is a great-grandmother. She still looks strong, but how old is she?"

Yannis smiled. "She told me she had her first child at seventeen, her first grandchild at thirty-six, and now she's still in her mid-fifties. She's like Anna. Children have been her life's work and she loves it."

"Younger than I thought. Well, if you're sure it wouldn't be too much for her, I would be happy to bring Rose along every day if that's what you're suggesting."

He took a deep breath. "Better still, why don't you move in?"

He found he was holding his breath now, not only because there was a big lorry with a large load of timber coming down towards him on this narrow bend but also because he'd finally got around to saying what he'd wanted to say for the past few weeks of this long hot summer.

"Wow, that was a close shave!" Cathy said as she tried to regain her composure. She'd tensed up as the lorry had rumbled towards them. But the child-care solution that Yannis had just come out with had been so spontaneous, so heartfelt that she was thrown into confusion at the implications of the situation she had to consider.

Yannis took one hand off the wheel as they reached the straight section of the road at the top of the hill and took hold of her hand, waiting for her reply. She looked down at the toy-like boats moored in the harbour for the night as she tried to calm herself. The lights had just come on, twinkling all the way down the road below her. The harbour looked like a toy town.

Everything was moving too fast for her. She needed more time to think – but under the circumstances she had to come to a quick decision.

"You're very quiet," he said, taking his hand away again in case it was clouding her judgement.

It wasn't a big decision, was it? He still couldn't understand what went on in Cathy's head half the time!

"Surely, it's the obvious solution. I mean, you've often stayed at home with me over the summer, haven't you? Sometimes with Rose, sometimes by yourself like last weekend."

She couldn't help herself smiling at the memory of last weekend. Anna had insisted she needed a complete break because she'd been working so hard. So when Yannis had suggested a weekend at home with him she'd jumped at the chance. And it had been truly paradise, just the two of them!

But one night was different from moving in

with all the implications of surrendering her independence. There was absolutely no guarantee that this was what he really wanted. She reasoned that he was such a good-hearted person he'd simply been thrust into a situation where he was feeling it his duty to help her out in an emergency. She shouldn't read anything into it.

His fingers had slid back to grasp hers. She told herself firmly now that she had to stick to the survival plan she'd made weeks ago. Take their relationship day by day. Don't expect anything to be permanent. Just enjoy the present.

"Well?" he asked.

"I think that would be the best solution to the problem," she said carefully. "But we should run it past Eleni and see what she thinks."

"I know already what Eleni will think," he said happily. "She'll be over the moon to have the two of you there all the time."

"Just temporarily," Cathy put in quickly. "One or two weeks, Anna said."

"Whatever," he told her, switching off the engine as they arrived at the end of Cathy's street. "I'll ask Petros to pick up you and Rose in the morning so you don't have a problem with the luggage. I've got an early start in Theatre tomorrow."

He got out of the car and came round to open her door.

"I won't be bringing much luggage," she said as she climbed out. "I won't be there for long."

"Bring what you like," he said easily, sensing that she was still worried about the situation and needed reassurance. "We're kitted out already for Rose, as you know, so it's just a case of a few clothes for the pair of you. Can you be ready by eight? When you've settled Rose in with Eleni, you can come along and start work. You're in Outpatients tomorrow, aren't you? I'll make sure you're covered until you arrived."

"Thanks a lot. You've been so helpful about this."

She looked up at him, wanting so much to be taken into his arms, to know that he wasn't just being dutiful towards her.

"Mama!" Anna had appeared in her doorway, holding Rose's hands so that she could walk a few steps towards her mother.

"Come to Yannis!"

He was holding out his arms towards the small girl, who was beaming with delight at the sight of her mother and her beloved Yanyan. He took a few steps towards her and she reached out to grasp his hands.

"Well done!" He lifted Rose up into his arms. "*Kali spera*, Anna. I'm so sorry to hear about your sister. Cathy and Rose are coming to stay over at my house until you get back."

Anna smiled. "That's good. I won't worry about them if they're over in Nimborio with you, Yannis."

Lying in the warm sun, stretched out on the shore at the end of Yannis's garden, Cathy was telling herself that however temporary her relationship with Yannis was she was certainly going to make the most of it.

She looked around her at the sparkling sea, the hills with the heat haze rising from them to burn away before it got as far as the blue, blue sky. If this wasn't paradise, what was? And to think, a couple of days earlier when Yannis had suggested she and Rose move in, she'd hesitated before coming to a decision.

After two days of being pampered and cared for she was feeling as if she was a completely different woman to the harassed individual she'd been before she'd moved in with Yannis.

Oh, she'd had to go into hospital and work during the day, but that was what she was trained to do and it always gave her a sense of satisfaction at the end of the day. And she often got whole weekends off, like today.

She turned on her side to look at Yannis stretched out beside her, and found her pulses racing at the sight of his sensual, virile body. Only hours before he'd held her in his arms and they'd made love again. The culmination of a wonderful night together.

"Two weekends in a row, Dr Karavolis," she murmured. "Are you sure you're not giving us preferential treatment?"

"What if I am?" he said huskily. "We've shouldered a heavy load this summer. Things are easing off now and I can afford to be generous with time off duty for deserving doctors like you and me who've toiled through the difficult weeks. You can look forward to more time off than you've had of late."

She gazed through her sunglasses up into the sky where the sunlight was filtering through the dense branches of the olive tree that provided shelter for them. This was surely where she belonged. But for how long? How long before the dream lifestyle ended? It couldn't go on like this for ever. Not in her experience of real life!

She was right to be cautious, to take life with Yannis one day at a time.

Yannis eased himself up on one elbow and looked down at her. "Do you fancy a swim?"

"Soon. I'm enjoying being lazy, doing nothing for a change."

"What time is Eleni bringing Rose back here?"

"They're having some kind of family lunch at her house. They all adore children in their family, as you know, and I think she wants to introduce Rose to them. It's a good thing Rose is a gregarious little girl. Large gatherings never faze her. I don't expect she'll be back until the end of the afternoon. Why? Were you thinking we could go out in the boat or something?"

He bent his head closer to hers and kissed her gently on the lips. "Actually, I was thinking more along the lines of 'or something'," he murmured against her parted lips.

His kiss deepened and she felt the wonderful waves of renewed passion coursing through her body, tingling, tempting, impossible to resist… And why should she? The timing was perfect, both of them ready to renew the intimacy they'd enjoyed throughout the night.

He sensed her arousal as he gently drew her to her feet, brushing the sand off her arms as he held her closely against him.

"Let's go back to bed," he whispered huskily.

She smiled up into his eyes. There was nothing she would like better than spending a few more blissful hours alone with him.

They went in through the kitchen door and made their way across the hall to the foot of the stairs. One hand round her waist and the other on the carved oak of the banister, Yannis frowned and pointed across to the ornate highly polished hall table.

"What's the matter?"

She felt a chill of apprehension running through her. Was she about to wake up from the dream? Had it been too good to be true after all?

"Maroula's photograph. It's gone." He paused before staring at Cathy in bewilderment. "Have you moved it?"

She could feel the anger rising up. To be accused of something she hadn't done, something she'd wanted to do but had resisted for so long, was unbearable.

"No, I haven't moved Maroula's photograph!"

She could feel herself trembling. "Not that one on the hall table or any of her other photographs that seem to be everywhere in this house."

"Cathy, I was only asking. It seemed so strange not to have it there in its usual place."

"Well, I think it's strange to have the place full of Maroula's photographs when you've brought me here as your...I don't know what I am when I'm here with you, surrounded by all these reminders of your first love!"

She sank down at the foot of the stairs as tears of frustration poured down her cheeks.

He sat beside her but not too close. Her body was rigid, set in a don't-touch-me attitude.

"I'd no idea you felt like that. I'd simply got used to the photo being there and I noticed that—"

"Eleni must have moved it," she said evenly.

"Why would she do that?"

"She told me she thought it was time all the photographs were put away."

He stood up and began to pace around the hall. "So you discussed me with her, did you?"

"It wasn't a discussion. She simply came out with her opinion."

"And you agreed with her?"

"Actually, I told her you would put the photos away when you were ready to move on."

"Let me get this straight. You think the photos being around signified that I wasn't ready to move on?"

"I don't know what to think any more. It certainly didn't help me to have them here as a constant reminder of your idyllic first marriage."

"It wasn't always idyllic," he said quietly. "In fact, on the day Maroula drove off to her parents' house we had a big row."

He was standing very quietly now, looking down at the space where his wife's photograph had been.

Cathy waited as she saw the look of anguish on his face, knowing she mustn't break the silence or he might never reveal what was troubling him.

"She accused me of being completely selfish, always putting myself first. She said I was too ambitious to take her needs into consideration. I told her I was working hard to make a good life for my family. I had to take part in the conference that weekend. But she wouldn't listen. She slammed out of the house…and I didn't stop her. I was too wrapped up in the work I had to do."

He paused. Cathy could hear the grandfather clock ticking near him. She remained silent, willing him to continue.

He took a deep breath. "The next time I saw her was at the hospital. I never got to say goodbye. I drew the sheet back from her face and told her I was sorry. But the awful guilt remained."

Cathy stood up and moved swiftly across the hall to reach her arms out to him. He drew her against him and they stood, motionless, together.

"Yannis you've got nothing to feel guilty about. You were doing what you thought was right for your family. You had a row about it. All couples have rows. You didn't know Cathy would die the next day. That's why we should…"

She stopped. How could she tell him what she was thinking?

"Please go on, Cathy," he said, holding her even more closely.

"I think all couples should make the most of what they've got," she said cautiously. "We don't know what's around the corner in life."

He drew her closer to him. "Cathy, you're so precious to me I couldn't bear to lose you. I can't imagine life without you any more. But whenever I try to find out what's really worrying you, you hold back on me. You've got to tell me what's making you afraid of being really open with me."

For a few moments she remained absolutely still in his arms, knowing it was make-or-break time. As she raised her eyes to his she saw an expression of such love that she knew she had to tell him everything.

She moved out of his embrace and took hold of his hand, leading him into the sitting room. "Let's sit down together and I'll try to explain."

He looked at her apprehensively as they sat side by side in separate armchairs by the open windows.

She fixed her eyes on the wonderful view across the water, the tops of the gentle waves twinkling in the sunshine. She gazed at Yannis who was waiting for her to open up to him.

"Yannis, I've given my heart to several men and had it broken. It started with my father, my own flesh and blood. I adored him. I thought he would be there for ever with me. But one day he just walked out and never came back. So my heart was broken for the first time."

She drew in her breath, trying to control the tears that were threatening.

Yannis remained absolutely still. He longed to take her in his arms but he sensed she wanted to continue now and tell him the whole story.

"Later, there were boyfriends who seemed charming and attentive, fun to be with. But I was always too trusting. They were never what they'd seemed at first. It always ended in tears. But when Dave came along I really felt I could trust him."

She paused before continuing. These were memories she'd like to forget. "I met him in a wine bar in Leeds. I was relaxing with a few girlfriends for the evening. He came across and asked if he could buy us some drinks. Then he sat down at our table. He singled me out from the start and I was utterly charmed by him. He asked if he could take me out for dinner the next evening.

"Over dinner he told me a pack of lies —and I believed him! He told me his wife had left him the year before, but actually nothing could have been further from the truth. She had no idea that he was seeing me behind her back, their marriage was solid as far as she was concerned. I later discovered that not only was he still married, he also had children."

"Cathy, I can't bear to think how you must have felt when you found out the truth." Yannis moved across and sat on the arm of her chair, reaching down to cradle her in his arms.

"It was a whole year before I did. He'd moved into my flat. He said he was a banker in London so he used to work away Monday to Friday. After a while he started going away on so-called business trips and I wouldn't see him for weeks at a time and…"

He held her close as she began to sob.

"And then, on two occasions he called out his wife's name in the night. Maggie, she was called. So when you started to say Maroula's name on the boat it brought it all back to me and just as I was beginning to trust you I couldn't help thinking you would be like all the other men in my life. I couldn't trust my own judgement where men were concerned. Eventually you would leave me. I was just too afraid to give myself to you completely. I had to hold something back, to plan for a future where there was just Rose and me so that—"

"No, no, that will never happen, my darling.

You are the love of my life now. Maroula will always be precious to me, but it doesn't diminish my love for you in any way. My feelings of guilt have absolutely vanished. And while I'll never forget Maroula, you are the centre of my life now. You were saying just now that couples should make the most of every moment together because you never know what's round the corner. Well, that's especially true of couples like us."

He took a deep breath. "Cathy, I've wanted to make the most of every minute of my time with you. But I sensed you were wary of making a commitment to me…and I don't blame you, after all you've been through. But if I wait until I think you might agree to…what I'm trying to say is… will you marry me?"

She lay back against the pillows, wondering if it had all been a dream. In a book she'd read as a child it had said that sometimes people would pinch themselves to make sure.

"Ow!"

"Cathy, what's the matter?" Yannis came into the bedroom and hurried across to the bed.

She smiled up at him. "It definitely works."

"What does?"

"The pinch test to see if you're dreaming or not. Try it on yourself."

He set the bottle of champagne down on the bedside table and still holding the clean glasses in one hand he reached out towards her, stroking the side of her face tenderly.

"I know I'm not dreaming," he said huskily. "The last few hours have been completely real to me. As soon as you gave me the answer to the question I've been wanting to ask you for so long, I knew I'd never felt so alive."

He opened the champagne, handed her a glass and climbed back in beside her.

"Here's to the beginning of our real partnership," he said, linking his arm through hers as they brought their glasses to their lips. "Let's make a pledge that we'll be together as a family for ever."

"A family for ever!" they said as they clinked their glasses.

"You know, Yannis, Rose was one reason why I was holding back. I could see how she loved you and you loved her and I didn't want to put her through what I'd been through. My mother would bring a new boyfriend home, I'd get to know him, become fond of him, then he'd disappear and I was heartbroken."

"Darling, that would never happen with me. I adore Rose. I feel as if she's my own daughter. I can't wait…" He broke off and smiled. "What I'm trying to say is I do hope we're going to add to our family."

Cathy smiled back. "Of course we are. Well, we can try anyway."

"That will be fun!"

Cathy sighed. "To think it took a row to bring us to our senses."

"It certainly cleared the air." He lay back against the pillows, his head close to hers.

"That was our first row. We should have had one sooner."

"How about instead we both speak our minds when there's something worrying us? Then we won't need to have rows when we're married. For instance, if you'd told me sooner that you were fed up with seeing Maroula's photos around the house, I'd have put them away ages ago. I put them on display when I first moved in. They were a source of comfort to me at first but after I met you the photos remained simply because I'd got used to them being in the same places."

His words were taking away any doubts that might have lingered about the sincerity of his proposal. She felt she'd never been so happy in her life as she listened to his husky, emotional voice.

"More and more, during the past few weeks I've come to value my present life more than my past. I haven't dreamed about Maroula for ages… but I've dreamed about you. The first time it happened I woke up to find you weren't there and I was longing to go back to sleep and get back into my dream."

She sighed. "I still feel as if I'm dreaming. I can't actually remember what I said when you asked me to marry you."

"You didn't speak for what seemed such a long time to me. You looked as if you'd been struck dumb. And when you finally put me out of my misery you were whispering so quietly that I had to ask you whether you'd said yes or no."

"For the first time in my life I'd been struck dumb. And don't look at me like that because it was true."

"I never thought you would be at a loss for words, but you really were. I was worried you might faint."

"Was that why you carried me up to your bedroom and—?"

"Our bedroom," he corrected. "I was hoping we could live here after we're married but if you prefer we start off somewhere new, I can—'

"I love this place. I'll make a few changes here and there but…"

"Talking of changes, I almost forgot."

"Where are you going?" She watched as he climbed out of bed.

He was opening his wardrobe. "I put them in here when I got back from Rhodes the other day. I was going to show you earlier today. Now, there's a coincidence!"

She was completely mystified. "Yannis, what are you…?"

"What do you think?" He swung round, holding a couple of silver-framed photographs in his hands. "I've been taking photos of you for weeks now. Sometimes you didn't even know, like on the boat with Rose… Look!"

He held out the lovely picture of mother and daughter that he treasured so much.

"I finally got around to having these two photos framed. I've discovered this excellent shop where they will make silver frames for your favourite pictures. I love this one where I asked you to look at the camera. You look so relaxed here."

"Yannis, I'd no idea you'd done anything with them! People take photos and forget about them, leave them in the camera or on their mobile."

"I couldn't forget these. I've got a whole boxful waiting to be framed. Very soon when we get loads of wedding photos we—"

He broke off as he heard voices downstairs.

"Eleni is back with Rose!" Cathy said, putting down her glass and leaping out of bed. She was pulling on her hastily discarded bikini and sarong which was lying on the floor together with Yannis's swimming trunks. "I'll go down and explain we were changing after our swim."

Yannis laughed. "Let's tell them the good news before we explain anything. Eleni will be so excited to be the first person to be invited to the wedding."

They linked hands as they went downstairs. "And Rose will be over the moon when I tell her she's going to be a bridesmaid," Cathy said, happily. "Even though she won't understand she'll realise that something wonderful is happening."

"The most wonderful event in my life."

"Mine too."

EPILOGUE

THEY'D chosen to have the wedding in the spring mainly because of Yannis's deep desire to adopt Rose so that she would be his daughter when they were married. He'd asked Cathy to put him in touch with Dave so they could arrange a meeting with a solicitor in London. It took several weeks to organise this but eventually, in the depths of an English winter, a meeting was arranged.

When Yannis got back from London, Cathy had been relieved to hear that Dave had been so amicable. He'd agreed that Yannis could adopt Rose. He'd explained that his wife still didn't know of the existence of his daughter. However, when Rose reached an age when she could understand that Yannis wasn't her biological father, she should be told the truth. If or when she asked to see Dave he would be happy to meet her. His wife would then learn of the existence of his daughter but he would deal with the consequences of that when it happened.

As Petros drove Yannis, Cathy and Rose back from the church to their house, the narrow road beside the water was lined with people calling out their good wishes to the happy couple.

Rose, firmly ensconced between the two of them, was waving madly. Above her head Yannis leaned across to Cathy.

"Happy?"

"What do you think? The church service was so moving. But I'm longing to get back home."

"Me too. I'll be especially happy when everybody leaves us by ourselves tonight."

Cathy gave a dreamy sigh. "Absolutely! But the feast that Eleni has prepared will be the finest wedding breakfast in the history of the world. Yannis, keep waving! We'll have plenty of time to ourselves tonight."

And tonight she would tell him her wonderful secret! Oh, she'd hugged it to herself ever since the test had confirmed her suspicions that morning. She hadn't dared to tell Yannis when they had to go through that long wedding service together. He would have been just too excited!

He was hoisting Rose onto his lap. "My beautiful daughter is my official waving person. She's doing a great job."

They were pulling into the drive now. Rose was allowed out so she could show off her beautiful bridesmaid dress to anybody who hadn't seen it. She twirled on the step in front of the front door and the photographers snapped madly.

"Bride and groom in front of their home!"

Cathy shook out the creases from her fabulous ivory silk gown, stepping carefully over the gravel in her impossibly high, strappy, elegant shoes. Yannis was holding her arm to make sure they made it to the top step.

They obliged with a couple of photos and then Cathy, catching sight of her mother in the crowd of guests, called out, "Mum! Come and have another photo taken with us."

"You can't be the mother of the bride," one of the photographers said. "You're much too young."

Cathy's slim, glamorous mother, radiant in an oyster satin suit, smiled at her daughter.

Cathy squeezed her mother's hand. "Sorry your new boyfriend couldn't make it. How's it going?"

"Well, as you know, I always live in hope but I'm never surprised if it goes wrong. One thing I'm certain of, though, you and Yannis are soulmates. Nothing will go wrong with this marriage. Absolutely rock solid you are. Take it from me…"

"Smile for the camera, please. Three generations of beautiful girls, grandmother, bride, bridesmaid…put the little girl in the centre…"

"Ah!" The guests assembled in front of the house voiced their approval of the lovely family scene.

"And now, bride and groom, just one more time, please!"

"We're going inside after this one," Yannis whispered as they obliged the photographers. "I thought we could perhaps go upstairs and change into something casual like…how about that new negligee you bought?"

"Later…not long now…"

Yannis was nestled against the pillows waiting for her when she came out of the bathroom, loosely fastening the belt of her new silk negligee.

"Wow!"

"Do you like it?" She gave a twirl.

"What?"

"This expensive negligee you bought me."

"Oh, yes. I was talking about what was in it,

though. Come a little closer so I can get a better view."

As she reached the side of the bed he reached out and with a deft flick of the hand removed the belt. The negligee hung loosely open now.

"Mmm, that looks much better. Better take it off so you don't crease it."

She smiled as she shrugged it to the floor, her body already tingling with anticipation of the night ahead. Climbing into bed, she snuggled against him.

"Would you like me to tell you a secret?"

"Only if you want to tell me. Is it good news or...?" He'd never seen her look so radiant.

"Cathy, It's not what I think it is...is it?" He was holding his breath as he waited for her answer.

"Well, that depends on what—"

"Are we going to have a baby? Are we...? Tell me, darling."

"We're going to have a baby, a little sister or brother for Rose."

"Oh, that's wonderful! I hadn't dared to hope. You've just made me the happiest man in the world! But, hey, are you sure?" His eyes twinkled mischievously.

"I did a test in the bathroom this morning. I'd

bought the most reliable testing kit because I was late with my period. I'm sure."

He drew her closer. "Don't you think we should make absolutely sure?"

She smiled provocatively. "How?"

"I'd hoped you'd ask that! Let me show you…"

MEDICAL™

Large Print

Titles for the next six months…

February

WISHING FOR A MIRACLE	Alison Roberts
THE MARRY-ME WISH	Alison Roberts
PRINCE CHARMING OF HARLEY STREET	Anne Fraser
THE HEART DOCTOR AND THE BABY	Lynne Marshall
THE SECRET DOCTOR	Joanna Neil
THE DOCTOR'S DOUBLE TROUBLE	Lucy Clark

March

DATING THE MILLIONAIRE DOCTOR	Marion Lennox
ALESSANDRO AND THE CHEERY NANNY	Amy Andrews
VALENTINO'S PREGNANCY BOMBSHELL	Amy Andrews
A KNIGHT FOR NURSE HART	Laura Iding
A NURSE TO TAME THE PLAYBOY	Maggie Kingsley
VILLAGE MIDWIFE, BLUSHING BRIDE	Gill Sanderson

April

BACHELOR OF THE BABY WARD	Meredith Webber
FAIRYTALE ON THE CHILDREN'S WARD	Meredith Webber
PLAYBOY UNDER THE MISTLETOE	Joanna Neil
OFFICER, SURGEON…GENTLEMAN!	Janice Lynn
MIDWIFE IN THE FAMILY WAY	Fiona McArthur
THEIR MARRIAGE MIRACLE	Sue MacKay

MILLS & BOON

MEDICAL™

Large Print

May

DR ZINETTI'S SNOWKISSED BRIDE	Sarah Morgan
THE CHRISTMAS BABY BUMP	Lynne Marshall
CHRISTMAS IN BLUEBELL COVE	Abigail Gordon
THE VILLAGE NURSE'S HAPPY-EVER-AFTER	Abigail Gordon
THE MOST MAGICAL GIFT OF ALL	Fiona Lowe
CHRISTMAS MIRACLE: A FAMILY	Dianne Drake

June

ST PIRAN'S: THE WEDDING OF THE YEAR	Caroline Anderson
ST PIRAN'S: RESCUING PREGNANT CINDERELLA	Carol Marinelli
A CHRISTMAS KNIGHT	Kate Hardy
THE NURSE WHO SAVED CHRISTMAS	Janice Lynn
THE MIDWIFE'S CHRISTMAS MIRACLE	Jennifer Taylor
THE DOCTOR'S SOCIETY SWEETHEART	Lucy Clark

July

SHEIKH, CHILDREN'S DOCTOR...HUSBAND	Meredith Webber
SIX-WEEK MARRIAGE MIRACLE	Jessica Matthews
RESCUED BY THE DREAMY DOC	Amy Andrews
NAVY OFFICER TO FAMILY MAN	Emily Forbes
ST PIRAN'S: ITALIAN SURGEON, FORBIDDEN BRIDE	Margaret McDonagh
THE BABY WHO STOLE THE DOCTOR'S HEART	Dianne Drake

MILLS & BOON®